Filmography

Shane Simmons

ISBN: 978-0-9952776-1-8

Filmography
Copyright © 2016 by Shane Simmons
All Rights Reserved.

Published by Eyestrain Productions
eyestrainproductions.com

I am a camera with its shutter open,
quite passive, recording, not thinking.

Christopher Isherwood,
Goodbye to Berlin, 1939

Forward

LOOK, FIRST OFF, before we go anywhere with this, I wanted to say how sorry I am. Sorry to the family, sorry to the fans, sorry to Basil himself. None of us meant for this to go quite so far, to spiral so out of control, and certainly not to end on the horrible note it did. I know this is going to sound completely fucked, but what we did was out of respect, admiration, affection. In our own, sad way, we had the best of intentions. This wasn't the epitaph we wanted to write.

With the footage in lockup, injunctions filed, lawsuits pending, and criminal charges aplenty, someone had to make a record of these events for posterity. There's been so much speculation, so much embellishment, so many lies, I wanted to get the facts out there. Maybe with the whole story in print, we might not come off as the despicable monsters we've been portrayed as in the media coverage and leaked police reports. Or maybe we will. But if I'm going to be despised and reviled, I'd rather it be for what I did, than for the stories and innuendo people invented which made a tale that was already plenty bad so much worse.

For what it's worth, here's my version of events. Try to reserve judgement. At least for as long as you can.

Act One

I T BEGAN, APPROPRIATELY enough I suppose, underground—in Charles Alexander Hardy's basement. Or, more accurately, his mother's basement, claimed as Chuck's and marked as his dominion by movie posters, movie memorabilia and, of course, movies. Movies on DVD, Blu-ray, HD-DVD, laserdisc and VHS. Beta was the only format of ages gone by that had no representatives in the collection, but that was only because Chuck had nothing to play them on. Obsolete as some releases were, Chuck had an excuse for keeping them all. Somehow, he always managed to find the handful of films that were never digitally transferred, or unearth commentary tracks that only existed on a defunct disc.

The central focus of the room was a fifty-inch widescreen extension of his penis. Countless hours had been sacrificed in the dark in front of this altar to the home-theatre experience. Chuck and his very select group of associates would sit on the ratty couch, or one of the ratty armchairs, and bathe in the plasma glow of the screen and the chorus provided by the 5.1 surround-sound system.

Apart from the equipment arranged to offer the best possible presentation of a vast reference library of film, Chuck also kept up to date with the means to make his own personal motion-picture projects. Since I'd known him, he'd collected a

Super-8, a Bolex, and various video cameras, tape and digital—at least one new model per year. At his behest, I had just run upstairs to grab his latest compact hi-def video camera from the dresser in his bedroom. It was fully charged and ready to go.

"Okay," I announced once I'd pulled focus and hit the record button, "rolling."

But Chuck, normally so talkative, so verbose, had nothing to say. He looked very far away even though he was sitting just a few feet in front of me.

"Chuck?" I prodded, after several long moments of static silence.

"Uh, yeah," he said, coming out of his stupor, "just gathering my thoughts."

"You have something you want to say on this momentous occasion?"

"I'm not sure."

"You're the one who told me to get the camera," I reminded him.

"Yeah. I guess I just wanted to record this moment. There's nothing to say, really."

"Well why don't you tell the viewers at home what's so special about it."

Chuck consulted the LCD display shining on one of his theatre components.

"Let's see," he said, noting how much time had elapsed. "It was about four minutes ago. It came on the news, just a little 'oh-by-the-way' at the end."

Chuck paused for effect before making the dire announcement.

"Basil Hendrich is dead."

"He was what, eighty-three?" I asked, trying to remember the details the anchor had read off the teleprompter obituary.

"And two months and fourteen days," specified Chuck, who knew all the pertinent biographical facts by heart.

Shooting Chuck in this manner felt like a testimonial, so I prompted him for more.

"Can you tell us who Basil Hendrich was?"

"Fuck, everybody knows who Basil Hendrich was, man."

"For the uninitiated," I suggested, aware that the rest of the world was not as immersed in retro pop culture as Chuck or the chosen ones who travelled in the same circles.

"Fuck them!" Chuck blurted out, addressing the camera directly. "If you don't know who Basil Hendrich was, I've got no time for you, you ignorant fuck!"

"Way to endear your audience."

Chuck settled down and continued the interview in a more civil tone.

"Basil Hendrich was the greatest screen actor ever," he declared solemnly.

"Ever," agreed Steve Coolidge from off-camera.

I pivoted in place to get Steve in the frame. He was sitting in the second torn and faded armchair on the other side of the room. Although he wasn't as upset about the news concerning Basil Hendrich, he agreed with Chuck's assessment of the late thespian's stature.

"In the entire history of cinema," Chuck added.

"Not Brando," said Steve.

"Fuck Brando!" answered Chuck.

"Not De Niro," said Steve.

"Fuck De Niro, and fuck his mole!"

"Not..." Steve tapered off, considering the list of giants.

"Who's a good one, Vince?" he asked, consulting my considerably inferior film knowledge.

"Bogart?" was the first name that leapt to mind, so I threw it into the fray.

"How's about Bogart?"

"Bogie's cool," conceded Chuck, "but he's no Basil."

"Pardon me for being one of the ignorant fucks," I interjected, apprehensive of what Chuck's reaction might be once he discovered I wasn't a member of the superfandom, "but what was he in? I don't think I ever saw one of his movies."

"Sure you have," Chuck told me. "Everybody has. Whether you know his name or not, you've seen his face a thousand times in a thousand different flicks."

Chuck got up abruptly and walked across the room to an end table in the corner. He pulled open a drawer and retrieved the framed photo inside. Normally it would have hung in a place of honour on the wall, but the glass was cracked and awaiting replacement after some careless manhandling. He brought it to me and stuck the eight-by-ten black-and-white glossy in my face. It was a head shot of a gaunt, aging actor, signed across the bottom in silver pen, "To Charles, fear the night, Basil Hendrich." I vaguely remembered seeing it before, one sample from Chuck's collection of autographed movie-star mementos. When it came to B- and C-level celebrities, it was amazing how much stuff you could get signed and personalized with mail-order and thirty bucks.

"Oh yeah, I know him," I declared upon seeing the familiar face. "Wasn't he in just about every horror movie ever made?"

"Basil was king," Chuck nodded. "The king of horror, science-fiction, and sometimes westerns. He played Dracula more times than anybody."

"Except Christopher Lee, right?" I felt compelled to correct.

"Well, yeah, of course," Chuck admitted.

"And John Carradine," Steve weighed in.

"Sure sure," agreed Chuck testily. This was film-school 101 to him. "Goes without saying. But after those guys, it was him."

"What was his last movie?" I asked.

> **Backslash 2** (2007) 103min. U.S.A. Director: Vince Todd, Cast: Trevor McNee, Tracy Dodge, Andrea Tennet, Markie Jones, Ella Pratt, Basil Hendrich. Unnecessary sequel to the tech-sector torture-porn hit from two years earlier. Another group of nubile web designers is preyed upon by a mysterious psychopath who stalks them on the Internet and plots their ironic (and gratuitously gruesome) fates. Marginally better than the original, which isn't saying much. Avoid. *½

Upstairs, in Chuck's bedroom, Steve read the results of a web search off a computer screen. A page was open, listing the complete and utter filmography of Basil Hendrich, cradle to grave or thereabouts.

"His final screen appearance was in *Backslash 2*," said Steve, reciting from near the bottom of the list.

"Seen it," Chuck felt obliged to confirm.

"Of course you have."

"He did a cameo as the innkeeper," Chuck elaborated. "Little nod to the fans, but not a very worthwhile movie."

Steve found a final credit at the very bottom of the page, noted "voice only."

"Technically, his very last film was that thing about the mouse—you know, the animated Disney-wannabe kiddie-pic that came out last year."

Chuck nodded sadly. "He did a lot of voiceover work towards the end. Not a high note to go out on."

"Actors take what pays the bills when their careers are winding down," said Steve, quick to make respectful excuses for the departed.

"Yeah, but some still manage to go out on a real cool movie," said Chuck. "Not necessarily good, but cool. Joan Crawford in *Trog*. Bela Lugosi in *Plan 9*. Veronica Lake got to feed Hitler's face to maggots in *Flesh Feast*. Total piece of shit, but that was so worth her coming out of retirement to do."

Steve had clicked a link to Basil Hendrich's obituary, one of dozens that had cropped up on all the media pages that covered entertainment news and gossip. As they did for so many old celebrities, they'd probably had an obituary on file for years. A few tweaks and it could be made ready to release at a moment's notice. This particular one had been updated to include details about the funeral. As it turned out, Hendrich had been dead a few days already. Being a lesser, largely forgotten movie star, the press release announcing his death had only gone out later the same week.

"It says here that services were held in his home town of Templeton," summarized Steve.

"The prodigal son returns," was my comment.

"Isn't that some dinky little truck stop just past Kingston?"

Hendrich was one of those secret Canadians who had made a career for himself in Hollywood and never looked back. It was where the money was. But apparently the roots of the maple tree ran deep, and Basil had wanted to be buried back in the home town he probably hadn't seen since he was a kid with stars in his eyes.

"If we'd known earlier, we could have gone down," I said.

"We still could," suggested Chuck.

The drive was hours away, but not tremendously far. It wouldn't even require a motel stay to get there and back to pay our respects.

"Your car, your call," said Steve.

We were game. There was nothing else on our agenda.

"I think a road trip is in order," announced Chuck. The pilgrimage was on.

> **Bad Boys Finish First** (2006) 92min. U.S.A. Director: Bradley Munson, Cast: Jenni Tarp, Bruce Phrennig, Tommy Armstrong, Pearl Gallos, Basil Hendrich, Hal Durring. Fluffy musical comedy starring a gaggle of teen idols you won't recognize if you're on the wrong side of 30. Some catchy tunes in this otherwise light and bland time-killer. Minimal sexual innuendo keeps it suitable for the kids. Numerous cameos from familiar faces and where-are-they-now celebs will keep mom and dad from being completely bored. **

I brought the camera along and continued to diligently document our impromptu voyage. With many gigs of space on multiple memory sticks, there was no excuse to stop recording. Even then, I only thought to resume the shoot four hours down the highway when we made a pit-stop at a roadside donut shop for refreshments and a bathroom break. The others were already inside as I doubled back to Chuck's compact shitbox to retrieve the camera and get a two-shot of the guys sitting at a window booth. Steve waved enthusiastically for the camera, Chuck extended his middle finger and pressed it to the glass. They were saying something, but I couldn't hear it over the din of heavy truck traffic rumbling by on both sides of the main artery.

By the time I joined them inside, Chuck was in the middle of one of his impassioned speeches—about movies, of course.

"I acknowledge it's a great film," he impatiently explained to Steve. "I'm just saying me, personally, I can't stand the fucking zither music. You take the same movie and give it a Waxman score or someone else like him and I'll watch it over and over again. But with the zither? I can only sit through that shit once. Sorry, but that's the way it is."

The references were over my head. They were probably discussing some dinosaur of cinema from long before any of us were born. Rather than try to get up to speed by provoking a tedious lecture, I interrupted the conversation by tossing a folded road map onto the table as I sat down.

"We're about fifty klicks out," I told them. "I figure we can ask a local-yokel for directions once we're in town."

Steve unfolded the sheet to confirm what I'd just said and found our approximate location along the blue line that marked the Trans-Canada Highway.

"What are you, a woman?" said Chuck derisively. "We're not stopping to ask for directions."

"Why the hell not?" asked Steve, who had had his fair share of experiences getting lost on the endless rural back roads of Ontario.

"We're just not, okay?" said Chuck. "We're in, we're out, we don't talk to anyone on the way."

"Antisocial much?" I asked Chuck.

Steve simply waved a dismissive hand at Chuck and returned his attention to the map.

"Aw, leave him alone," he cautioned me. "We're lucky he's even talking to us. Remember when Don Knotts died? He wouldn't answer his phone for a week."

I thought that reminder might provoke a defence from Chuck, but he said nothing, opting instead to stare into his coffee, deep in thought.

> **Page Turner Red** (2004) 132min. U.S.A. Director: Chad Torrence, Cast: Ben Jacobson, Carrie Dwight, Arnold Colsack, Jim Desmond, Annie Prudhomme, D.J. Jaz, Basil Hendrich. Movie-nerd tropes and glib one-liners fill the running time of this smarmy, winking in-joke of a film. Hipster director Torrence wears his genre cred thin after the first hour. Amusing enough if you're on the same wavelength, everyone else beware. Scene-stealing ham Basil Hendrich makes a welcome return in a small, but memorable role—his first after a nine-year absence from the big screen.
> ***

We found our exit an hour past the donut-and-toilet rest stop. Steve was in the back offering occasional directions that amounted to little more than "left" or "right." I sat shotgun with the camera and pointed the lens out the open passenger window as the car passed through a gate and wound its way around the twisting, scenic road of a small-town cemetery. This was the final destination of generations of Templeton residents who had been born there, raised there, and never escaped. Basil had escaped, yet somehow specified a wish to return. I guess there's no place like home, even if you're too dead to know you've come back at last.

Many of the gravestones were washed white by the years and the weather, with inscriptions that were left barely legible. These graves covered local history going back as far as the early days of Upper and Lower Canada, before politics and paperwork knitted the country together into a cohesive whole. Steve folded up the road map and leaned forward between the two front bucket seats so he could survey the grounds. He stuck his arm out between Chuck and me, pointing at the rows of fresher graves.

"That looks like where they're planting the newbies these days," he said.

"Yeah," Chuck agreed. "This is it."

Chuck was intensely focused on the plots ahead as he pulled the car over to the shoulder of the narrow road and parked. The three of us spilled out. Chuck went around to the back of the car and popped the trunk.

"Go on," he told us. "I'll be there in a minute."

Steve and I forged ahead, searching from marker to marker until we found Basil Hendrich's tombstone. It was easy to spot.

The newest grave in the cemetery was still buried under a pile of flowers and condolences.

"There he is," said Steve with a certain sense of awe.

"Wow," I agreed. "Brush with greatness."

I could hear Chuck's footsteps on the dry grass, approaching from the road.

"Chuck, you want to say a couple words?" Steve asked.

"Start digging," were the words Chuck chose.

A pair of shovels landed in front of us on top of the freshly filled grave and its floral blanket. We turned around and saw Chuck stepping up, brandishing a third.

"Huh?" said Steve, which was the best question he could come up with in the moment.

"Are you crazy?" was my more pointed attempt at a relevant query.

"Yeah, man," agreed Steve. "These are snow shovels."

Chuck began clearing the flowers and wreaths from the grave, carelessly tossing them to one side or the other.

"I never got to meet him," he said. "I want to see him in person."

"This isn't a book signing or a photo op," Steve reminded him. "The guy's dead."

"Then I'm not going to come across as some pain-in-the-ass fanboy. Dig!" insisted Chuck.

Steve hesitantly took up one of the shovels. He looked back at me for support and then to Chuck for confirmation. Chuck sharply nodded his chin at the grave and said no more. Reluctantly, Steve scooped up the first shovelful of dirt and cast it aside. Chuck joined him a moment later, digging with far more vigour.

After a few stabs at the earth, Chuck looked back at me and growled, "You too, Mr. Cinéma vérité."

I turned off the camera and set it down in exchange for the third shovel.

> **Deadly Shadows** (1998) 100min. U.S.A. Director: Sandra Snoddard, Cast: Rebecca Farns, Greg Kessler, Carlos Senza, Basil Hendrich, Ilsa Boyle, Donald Franz. Trashy woman-in-peril thriller that's little more than a time-slot filler for late-night TV with all-too-obvious fade-outs for commercial breaks. Attractive, successful D.A. is relentlessly menaced by a shadowy knife-wielding stalker. Is it an old case come back to haunt her, or her handsome new lover? Who cares? Unfortunately this direct-to-cable production can't deliver on the sex and violence front enough to make it memorable trash. **

I switched the camera back on about twenty minutes later. By then the grave had been exposed and we were all sweaty and dirty. Chuck inspected our handiwork with satisfaction. The casket lid was visible at the bottom of the hole we had excavated and Steve was prying at the corners with his shovel, trying to dislodge it. With the sound of cracking wood, the lid finally came loose and he was able to swing it open.

Chuck offered his hand and pulled Steve out of the grave. Together we stood on the edge of the pit we'd dug and looked down into the abyss. Six feet below us we beheld the tall, lanky, distinguished character actor lying in state on a bed of crisp white silk. I pointed the camera into the hole to capture the moment. It was the first time a motion-picture camera had been directed at the man since his semi-retirement into voice acting. There was no motion to capture. Basil Hendrich was as still as the grave he occupied.

We stared for a long moment that went on and on. The morticians had done a good job. Basil's corpse looked like a realistic waxwork of himself.

"Okay, there," said Steve at last, breaking the reverent silence, "you've met him. Can we fill this hole in again before we get busted by the groundskeeper?"

Instead of responding, Chuck jumped down into the open grave.

"Look, Chuck, I know you were, like, totally in love with the guy and everything. But we're not burying you with him."

Chuck ignored Steve's comment and barked an order.

"Get his feet," he said, "I got this end."

"Say what?" asked Steve.

"He's coming with us."

"You're out of your fucking head!" I told him in disbelief.

But after only a few seconds of internal debate, Steve jumped back into the hole alongside Chuck and grabbed the cadaver's legs.

"You're both out of your fucking heads!"

"Maybe," shrugged Steve, "But it'll make an amusing anecdote one day."

"For who? The prison psychologist?"

"No one's going to prison," insisted Chuck.

"It's not like we're committing a felony," Steve weighed in with his best legal advice. "This is more of a misdemeanor. Suspended sentence, tops."

"This is grave robbing!" I reminded them.

"It's not grave robbing," said Chuck.

"Okay, technically it's grave robbing," he added after a swift moment of reflection, "but don't think of it like that. This is a rescue mission. We're rescuing Basil from the worms."

He had the corpse by the shoulders. With Steve working the legs, they soon heaved the body of Basil Hendrich out of its not-so-final resting place.

After much struggle and awkwardness, all of which I dutifully recorded, Chuck and Steve were able to cram the body into the back seat of the car. Steve got in next to the corpse, leaving me to film from the front. Chuck got behind the wheel and pulled away, looping back to the town road by the circuitous path of the cemetery.

"This is totally fucking insane," I tried to protest.

Chuck ignored me and asked Steve, "How's he doing?"

Steve was staring at the corpse they had just forced into a sitting position in the back seat. He seemed morbidly starstruck.

"Still dead," Steve confirmed.

Chuck was running on nervous energy. His foot was heavy on the gas as he sped us out of the cemetery.

"Oh God, oh God, oh God, oh God," was the mantra I repeated to myself.

"Slow down, Chuck," Steve yelled from the back. "You're gonna kill us all!"

As we peeled around a corner, I spotted a man in overalls cresting one of the rolling hills of the graveyard. This was the feared and anticipated groundskeeper we had expected to discover us as we dug. He watched our speedy departure from his purview with suspicion, but did nothing to stop us.

"Oh God, oh God, oh God, oh God," I repeated anyway, hiding my face and failing to act casual.

A moment later and we were through the gates. Chuck raced out into the middle of the main drag, cutting through traffic and heading for the city limits.

> **Pearls of Wisdom** (1995) 93min. U.S.A. Director: Todd Randolph, Cast: Eddie Simone, Beverly Kamp, Basil Hendrich, Toby Gallib, Kobo Sante, Bobby Best. Young, out-of-their league treasure hunters consult a salty old seadog (Hendrich looks tired) on how best to recover a fortune that lies at the bottom of the ocean. Nefarious local mobsters want a cut, toothy local sharks want a bite. Low-rent adventure gets lost at sea. **

We were in the parking lot of another, identical donut shop along the highway. It was so similar, if could have easily been the exact same one as earlier except for the fact that it was on the opposite side of the road, servicing east-bound traffic.

Chuck and Steve were already inside. I was getting organized with the camera, swapping batteries, checking the space on the memory chip. I looked into the empty back seat of the car and knew this was a terrible idea, getting worse.

My grave-robbing companions were sitting at the same table as they had occupied at the twin donut franchise a short time ago. As I videoed them through the window, it might have been a different take of exactly the same shot with only one minor difference. The corpse of Basil Hendrich was now sitting alongside them. He was propped up in his seat, bolt upright, his features frozen, his eyes clamped shut.

"Good fucking Lord," I muttered to myself and entered the restaurant.

Inside, I found Chuck back on his soapbox, sounding off about another one of his film theories. I don't know if he was in denial about what he'd just done, or merely had a short attention span.

"So they install this new mechanical butter churn," Chuck explained, "and everyone's skeptical. But they get it going, and all these peasants are watching in anticipation, and finally liquid butter starts spurting out of the thing. And it's splashing over here, and it's splashing over there, and it's splashing all over the ugly old Russian chick's face and she's beaming like it's the greatest moment of her life."

Steve nodded knowingly, picturing the scene. Chuck stabbed an insistent finger into the tabletop for emphasis.

"Fuck *Potemkin*. Fuck *Nevsky*. It all comes down to *The General Line* in 1929. That's when Sergei Eisenstein, communist propaganda pioneer, gave us his greatest achievement— cinema's first cumshot. Go see it for yourself. It's the most pornographic industrial film ever made."

"I'll take your word for it," said Steve.

I sat down at the table opposite Basil, who rested stiffly in his plastic chair, head tilted back, jaw slightly agape, looking quite unpleasantly dead. I felt obliged to interrupt the film-studies lecture.

"Guys, what the fuck did we stop in here for?"

"Donuts," explained Steve.

"Coffee," added Chuck.

"Someone's going to see us!"

"Of course people are going to see us," said Chuck. "We're sitting right here in front of them."

"With a dead body!"

"They don't know he's dead."

"Don't know? Fucking look at him!"

"He looks pretty dead there, Chuck," Steve agreed.

"You think anyone's going to notice? Everyone here has their nose stuck in a smartphone or a cappuccino. To them we're just four guys sitting at a table."

The light was fading and the restaurant clientele was sparse, but I felt justified in my concern.

"They must have seen you carry him in."

"It's nighttime," replied Chuck. "He's sleepy."

We were approached by a bleary-eyed waitress who was at the end of her shift and must have been on her feet all day. She hardly acknowledged any of us, Basil least of all. Her eyes never left her order pad.

"What can I get you?" she mumbled.

"Coffee. Black," said Chuck.

"Coffee and a double chocolate twist," said Steve.

"Uh, I'll have a raisin muffin," I said, stealing a quick glance at the menu on the wall.

"And him?" asked the waitress. She hadn't even bothered to look at Basil, but her heightened waitress radar had detected there were four customers seated at her station.

"He'll have an espresso," Chuck told her.

Steve, seated next to Chuck, gave him a sharp elbow in the ribs. But the waitress wandered away a moment later without noticing anything amiss. Chuck giggled.

"Fucking asshole," I hissed at him.

"What are you doing ordering a light snack for the stiff?" asked Steve.

"He looks like he could use a pick-me-up."

"Real funny," I said.

"Shut up, I'll drink it."

"You're gonna get us caught, you keep up that shit," Steve said.

"Caught? Who's going to catch us?"

"The manager," I suggested. "The manager will throw a fucking fit if he sees we brought a dead body in here."

"The manager won't say shit," Chuck assured us. "The health board would shut his ass down so fast."

"Well maybe I like being a repeat customer here," I told him, "so knock it the fuck off."

"Chill okay? I told you pussies, nobody's gonna recognize..."

Chuck was cut off by a woman who had just come over from a neighbouring table to take a closer look. She had been staring for some time while trying not to look like she was staring. But at last she had mustered the courage to say something.

"Oh my God, is that...?" She tapered off before she could complete her sentence, but it was obvious it was the deceased at our table who had caught her attention.

We all froze, sure we'd been exposed. But the look on her face was one of delight, not horror. In that moment we realized she was a fan—old enough to have seen Basil in plenty of movies before his career took a turn for the obscure.

Steve slid over and put his arm around Basil, proudly declaring, "It sure is."

"Basil Hendrich?" asked the fan, hoping she had identified the correct star and not some lookalike.

"In the flesh," said Chuck.

"And the bones," I commented grimly and got a kick under the table from Chuck.

"I thought he was dead," the fan blurted out, and again we were sure we were done.

"I heard he died a good ten, fifteen years ago," she finally said when we failed to come up with any response.

"You're probably thinking of Vincent Price," Chuck corrected her.

"Or Peter Cushing," added Steve.

"That must be it," she nodded knowingly. So many titans, sadly departed.

The fan lingered a moment longer, embarrassed to ask what was really on her mind.

"You don't suppose...?"

"What?" asked Chuck.

"No, I couldn't," she said, waving him off.

"Tell us," Steve encouraged.

Reluctantly, she produced a disposable camera from her bag.

"Do you think I could get a picture with him?"

"You and Basil?" I asked, masking my dismay.

"Would he mind?"

Chuck and Steve exchanged a look and a nod.

"No, he wouldn't mind," Steve told her as he got up from his seat to let the fan slide in next to Basil. He took the camera from her and lined up a shot.

The fan leaned in closer and struck a pose, but she could tell something wasn't quite right with the celebrity. He hadn't moved or said a word to her and it was starting to look suspicious.

"Is he all right?" she asked with a look of genuine concern.

"Oh sure," said Chuck. "He's just in character."

"He's a long-time proponent of The Method," Steve clarified.

"We've been helping him rehearse for a cameo role in the next Romero *Living Dead* movie. They're shooting in Toronto again," said Chuck.

"So far he's got the dead part down pat," said Steve, and ended the discussion with an abrupt, "Smile!"

The fan leaned in again and fashioned a winning smile on command. Steve snapped a picture and the flash went off.

"Oh, Mr. Hendrich! You're such a card," said Steve to the corpse at the table.

The fan looked at Basil, but he remained unchanged.

"What happened?" she asked.

"He made a funny face just when I was taking the picture. You'll see when you get these developed," Steve said as he handed the camera back to her.

Chuck confided to the fan in a low voice behind his cupped hand, "I think he likes you."

The fan responded in an equally low voice so Basil wouldn't overhear the exchange.

"Isn't he married?"

"Not anymore, technically."

Basil Hendrich had been separated from his third wife for many years. She lived in a villa in Spain and probably hadn't even heard she was a widow yet.

"Don't you think he's a little old for me?" asked the fan, who was considerably younger but not exactly farm-fresh herself.

"He promises not to get any older," Chuck told her.

"Now, Mr. Hendrich, behave yourself," Steve admonished.

The fan looked at Basil again to see what she was missing, but he remained as unchanging as a slab of stone.

"What's he doing?"

"He's just acting silly," said Steve. "You keep missing it."

"I think he's shy," Chuck told the fan.

"Him, shy?" she replied. "He's a star."

"I guess fame and fortune doesn't go to everyone's head," said Steve.

"He's always been a class act that way," agreed Chuck.

"Well thanks for the picture, Mr. Hendrich," said the fan, rising from the table. "It was nice meeting all of you."

The fan turned around and started back to her own table, but she paused after a few steps and rushed back. Stretching across us, she stuffed a business card into Basil's breast pocket.

"Call me," she whispered softly in his ear.

Blushing at her own forwardness, the fan hurried back to her seat, collected her jacket, and went to the cash to pay her bill.

Our waitress returned a moment later and mechanically plunked down our order of coffee and snacks. Once she was gone, Steve fished the fan's card out of Basil's pocket. He took a moment to read it. Apparently she worked in real estate.

"Son of a bitch is room temperature and he still pulls more pussy than I do," said Steve.

He tossed the card across the table. It landed in Chuck's coffee and sank into the cup. Chuck pulled the dripping slip of card stock out of his drink.

"You mind?"

Chuck gave the card a flick, making sure to spatter Steve with coffee droplets, before tossing it onto our pile of discarded cream and sugar packets. The three of us snickered and laughed like boys misbehaving in grade school.

> **Fantasy Camp Party** (1993) 106min. U.S.A. Director: Frank Shriff, Cast: Gene Switch, Ellen Wessle, Paul Sweeney, August Barnes, Trevor Wick, Basil Hendrich, Angela Ribbard. Bargain-basement erotica is just another boob-jiggling sex comedy for arrested-adolescent males. Buddy baseball fans attend fantasy camp and play with a lot more than bats and balls. Full of forgettable young faces on naked bodies and a handful of old famous faces who (mercifully) keep their clothes on. *

We waited until it was completely dark out before taking Basil back to the car. As night fell, the lot started to fill up with regulars and passing truck drivers looking for a caffeine fix to keep them going for the next leg of their route. With Chuck and Steve keeping the body wedged between them in a more-or-less vertical position, no one gave us a second look.

The closer we got to home with our famous cargo, the more we realized there was no master plan—or at least no plan that Chuck had shared with us.

"Hey Chuck," said Steve after a long stretch of road and silence, "I'm enjoying this little corpsejacking as much as anyone, but how much longer are we going on this joyride of the dead?"

"I've been thinking about that," said Chuck, stealing a glance at our guest in the rear-view mirror. "Vince, how much of this have you been taping?"

I'd been running the camera on and off at irregular intervals, but hadn't documented anything more intriguing than passing landmarks for the past hour. I turned it back on and pointed it at Chuck.

"Okay, rolling again. What's up?"

"I'm just asking. In total, how much since before we dug up Basil?"

"Fifteen, twenty minutes maybe. Why?"

"You know, if we keep going, we could have a feature in another hour."

"Eighty minutes," I nodded. "That's a feature film."

"Pretty short," Steve agreed, "but it would count."

"Credits would stretch the run time," I suggested, seeing where Chuck was going with this line of thinking.

"And it would count as the last Basil Hendrich film."

"Well, yeah, I guess," said Steve. "But you're not going to see it written up in anybody's Movie and Video Guide or anything."

"Why not?"

"Because we're the only ones who know about it," said Steve, stating the obvious.

"Not if we show it to people."

"Like who?" I asked, suspicious that Chuck wasn't regarding what we were shooting in the same home-movie light I was.

"We could do the film-fest circuit," Chuck fantasized, "Just submit a cut and see what happens. Most of them will take anything if you've got a name star in it."

"And I suppose it wouldn't matter you were submitting incriminating evidence that was just going to land our asses in jail?"

This dose of reality came from Steve in the back, but Chuck was way ahead of him. The gears had been turning in his head as he'd stared at that long boring stretch of twin-lane pavement that bisected the wilderness between towns.

"If it sets us up in the film business? Hell, I could do fourteen months and parole for that kind of a foot in the door."

I saw Chuck's long-held dreams converging. Meeting his idol, working with him, and breaking into the industry that had held him in its thrall for so many years. It made perfect, horrible sense in Chuck's world.

"The buzz would be huge," he continued, and I knew he was pitching us like we were executive moguls sitting behind a desk in Hollywood, waiting for someone—anyone—to bring us a hit. "Everybody would be dying for us to get paroled just to see what crazy shit we'd do next."

Steve and I had been privy to Chuck's idle talk about his calling in show business before. Perhaps we'd even joined in from time to time. Wouldn't it be nice? Wouldn't it be fun? I never took it seriously.

"Chuck," I told him, "you can't make a feature film out of this."

But Chuck was already fixated on his half-baked idea and he was willing to defend it.

"Why can't I?" he asked.

He sounded confrontational, like he was looking to pick a fight with anyone out to talk sense to him. I tried a different approach.

"What the hell do you know about making movies?"

"I've made movies," Chuck said, like we should all have been aware of this fact.

"Like shit you've made movies," said Steve.

"I've made five or six movies," Chuck informed him.

"You're a pathetic liar."

"Name one," I prompted.

Chuck didn't hesitate. "*The Monster of Tarkon*," he said, like we would both know the title and feel shame for not thinking of it immediately.

There was only the briefest of pauses before Steve and I both burst out laughing.

"I must have missed that one," I said after regaining my composure. "I don't remember ever seeing it on the dollar-rental shelf."

"I'll show you," said Chuck, whose smug self-assuredness never wavered in the face of our openly mocking him.

Ginormous (1991) 97min. U.S.A. Director: Ogden Demers, Cast: Darleen Chadwick, Frank Noble, Bob Sawyerson, Basil Hendrich, Nolton James, Bonny Paolo. One of the last of the '80s-style creature features tries to hop

on the bandwagon after it's left town. Small
resort is menaced by a big monster. Pre-CGI
special F/X have a certain charm in retrospect
and get the job done. If only as much could
be said about the story and performances. *½

We were seated at the kitchen table in Chuck's house. It was
nearly midnight and Chuck's mom was down for the night.
After much digging, in the attic, in the basement, in the
crawlspace, Chuck had at last assembled his ancient Super-8
projector. Using the refrigerator as the largest available white
screen, he projected a roll of film he'd retrieved from a bin
containing several dozen home movies. They were all still in
their yellow developer boxes from when they came back in
the mail from the lab many years earlier.

Cast on the side of the fridge was a hand-drawn title card
for *The Monster of Tarkon*. What followed was a primitive work
of claymation with a Plasticine monster rampaging through a
sci-fi set of aluminum foil and painted toilet-roll tubes.

Steve shook his head in sad disbelief.

"This is so retarded."

"Shut up," Chuck told him, "I was twelve."

Climaxing with a special-effects miracle of hand-scratched
film, one of the spacescape towers shot the stop-motion monster, destroying it. The entire opus lasted a little under three
minutes and ended with a few final seconds of credits attrib-
uting the writing, directing, producing, lighting, set design and
animation to Charles Alexander Hardy.

There were a few other reels Chuck insisted on showing
us that followed his fledgling movie career into a Film Production course he once took in college. The content ranged

from childish genre tropes to pretentious teen angst. It was all amateur-hour crap, nothing to suggest we had an auteur on our hands. But Chuck had made his point. He'd made films before. They might have been terrible, but they allowed him to win that argument on a technicality.

Basil Hendrich was in the basement, sitting on the couch, dead to the world and facing an equally dead television set. We'd snuck him into the house under the cover of darkness. Only a single porch light had threatened to expose our late-night escapades to nosy neighbours, but even the nosy neighbours were in bed at that hour.

After Chuck's 8mm film fest, we all sat down in the available screening-room seating and observed our guest. I ran the camera, though there was nothing to capture but the stillness of a disturbed grave.

"So there he is," I said, focusing on the star of Chuck's new motion-picture project.

"There he is, all right," he agreed.

"Mr. Director, your star is delivering a rather wooden performance," said Steve.

"Maybe you could talk motivation with him," I suggested.

My sarcasm wasn't lost on Chuck, but he was game. He crouched down next to Basil like a director confiding in his temperamental diva. I closed in for a tight two-shot.

"Mr. Hendrich," he began. "Can I call you Basil?"

Chuck took the silence as consent.

"Basil, in this scene you're playing a freshly dug-up corpse. So I want you to clear your mind and think dead thoughts. You're dead, your life is over, you're not aware of anything, you're not doing anything, you're past all that. Now take a deep breath—better yet, don't breathe at all."

Chuck commended his actor when he received no response, "Right, that's perfect."

He backed off to leave Basil alone in my shot.

"Hold that moment," he instructed. "And...inaction!"

I kept rolling as nothing at all unfolded in front of me.

"Cut!" Chuck shouted from off-camera.

But I didn't cut. I merely took a step back so I could get Chuck and Steve in the shot with Basil.

"That was brilliant," I critiqued.

"He's never been better," agreed Steve.

> **Mondo Carnage** (1983) 86min. U.S.A. Director: uncredited, Cast: none. Ill-conceived throwback to the mondo genre of the '60s, reborn to capitalize on the direct-to-video market of the '80s. Mostly just a collection of horrible accidents and mishaps (some of them apparently fatal) captured on tape and collected here for ghouls. Voice-of-doom genre star, Basil Hendrich, collects a paycheque for narrating this odious piece of filth. BOMB

As inevitably happened in Chuck's basement, we ended up watching television. Chuck paid homage to our guest of honour by cracking out a season-one box set of a television show Basil had signed on for back when film roles were few and far between. It was one of those career lulls that often forced movie stars to go slumming on the boob tube. But the show, beneath him or not, developed enough of a cult following to make an aging character actor marketable again. The offers that came his way in the wake of his foray into the network less-than-prime-time wasteland were never up to the standards he had once enjoyed, but he jumped on them when they came at last. The small screen could not contain the thespian power-house that was Basil Hendrich. Besides, his TV show got slaughtered when some idiot in programming put it up against two back-to-back hit sitcoms. It was cancelled soon after, never to be renewed for a fourth season.

"Is this the one where they find out they're on some alternate Earth at the end?" asked Steve as we began the third episode of our marathon.

"That's, like, ninety percent of all the episodes," said Chuck.

"It was a pretty crap show, even for the eighties,'" I said, remembering all too well why I never caught it as a syndicated rerun.

"Too bad he didn't get another series after this one," said Steve.

"Fuck TV," said Chuck. "He was a movie star."

Chuck turned to Basil and apologized.

"Don't get me wrong, Basil, you were great on this show."

"At least he had a speaking part."

"What's that supposed to mean?" Chuck asked Steve.

"I mean here we are with one of the most distinctive baritone voices in cinema history and he's not saying shit in our movie."

"You can hear him right now on the tube. Vince, get a shot of the set," said Chuck, motioning for me to turn the camera towards the television screen.

"If we're releasing this, don't we need to pay someone to show a clip from *Nebula Hunters*?" I asked.

"Just point the camera, I'll worry about buying the rights later. How much could a two-second clip of a crap show cost?"

"More than you have," Steve chimed in. "This film of yours has a budget of exactly zero dollars. Besides, it's no fair stealing somebody else's footage."

"I gotta tell you, Chuck, your efforts to pad this out to feature-length are coming up short."

At Chuck's behest, I'd wasted more than enough memory space recording us sitting in the dark with Basil, lit only by the images of his past forgotten glories. Chuck seemed oblivious to the amount of filler we'd shot so far.

"How so?" he asked in all seriousness.

"We're not doing anything!"

"We're watching television," Chuck protested.

"Exactly!"

"With a dead guy," added Steve, pointing out our one and only hook.

"Yeah, but who cares?" I said, shutting off the pointless camera coverage of this non-event. Our casual indifference to what we were doing was starting to get to me. Maybe it was the late hour, or the company, but I was starting to feel ill.

"This is the most fucked-up thing ever," I muttered in despair.

There was a long silence as we all contemplated whether this was, indeed, the most fucked-up thing ever. Leave it to Steve to come up with a relevant point of trivia.

"Actually, no," he said. "The same thing happened to Chaplin."

"Charlie?" I asked.

"'Charles' if you please," Chuck corrected me with the preferred film-buff formality for the legend of silent cinema.

"He got dug up and dragged around town too," Steve informed me.

"And Elvis," Chuck added.

"Elvis as well?" Steve didn't know about that one.

"Yup. Which you think would put the rumours of him not being dead to rest, but you can't talk sense to the devout Elvis worshippers."

"Okay," I conceded, "so this is the third most fucked-up thing ever."

"It's probably happened a lot more often than people like to admit," Chuck speculated.

"Digging up dead celebrities was all the rage in the seventies," said Steve.

"Like streaking and bell bottoms," agreed Chuck.

Neither of them was selling me on the idea that this was, in any way, normal behaviour. But it led naturally enough to the next question. A question I will forever regret asking.

"Well once they dug them up, what the hell did they do with them?"

Steve and Chuck turned to look at each other. They both knew the answer. And it was just then that a terrible understanding passed between them and damned us all.

Act Two

THE NEXT MORNING we reconvened at one of the rare public phone booths still in operation in the neighbourhood. It sat outside a local convenience store and was used by no one but taggers and vandals who alternately painted over the glass panels and broke them. Amazingly, the phone-company relic still worked, and for the ridiculously overpriced fee of fifty cents you could make a local call. Feed it more change and you could get limited long-distance service.

"I still say one of us should have stayed to guard the stiff," Steve protested. "If your mom comes downstairs and sees what her baby boy brought home..."

"The woman collects sleeping-pill prescriptions," Chuck assured him. "She'll be out till noon."

Chuck stepped into the booth and picked up the receiver.

"I'm more concerned about this call being traced," I said.

"No one's going to trace the first call," said Chuck. "As long as a star-sixty-nine doesn't give them my home phone number, we're good."

"Yeah, but it could still point them at this phone booth," said Steve, who was starting to share my concern.

"A booth that just happens to be around the corner from your house with our fingerprints all over it," I added, lifting the camera to get a shot of my hand poking the glass of the booth repeatedly with my index finger.

Chuck fed the coin slot a couple of quarters and punched three numbers on the pad.

"Would you two quit it?" he said. "Everyone's going to know it was us as soon as we release the film anyway."

Someone picked up the line and Chuck spoke into the phone receiver, "Hello? Directory assistance please."

Chuck let the booth doors swing shut, blocking Steve and me out.

Steve yelled through the glass, "Yeah, but it would be nice if we didn't get busted until after we wrap principal photography!"

Left outside, looking in, Steve and I spoke alone for the first time since Chuck had led us down this grim path.

"Steve, seriously. What the fuck are we doing?"

Steve was almost as crazy as Chuck sometimes, but I usually relied on him to be the voice of reason. Or at least the voice of lesser insanity.

"It's cool, okay," he said.

"It is not cool! We are way past misdemeanor here. I don't think this even counts as a felony anymore. This is, like, some international extortion ring. We're going to have multiple law enforcement agencies fighting over who gets to throw us in prison."

"No one's going to get the cops involved, don't worry," said Steve. "Chuck's got it all worked out."

"Chuck's a fucking maniac," I told him. "You know that, right?"

"Well, yeah. But you stick by your friends, you know?"

"Whatever," I said, unconvinced.

"Just remember," he added, "if this shit goes down wrong, we pin it all on him."

It was the first reasonable thing I'd heard in the last twenty-four hours.

Chuck poked his head out a moment later.

"Got it!" he announced.

"Ready with the tape?" Steve asked.

From his collection of outdated technology, Chuck pulled a small tape recorder out of his pocket. It was the perfect device to pair with the nearly defunct phone booth. A microphone attachment with a suction cup dangled on the end of a wire plugged into the side. Chuck licked the cup and affixed it to the earpiece of the receiver.

"Yeah," he said. "We can splice in the other end of the conversation in post."

Chuck listened to his connection being made and put the phone to his ear. I closed in for a tight shot. The built-in microphone on the camera couldn't hope to pick up the voice on the other end, but I was close enough to hear it with my own ears. Steve leaned in to eavesdrop as well.

"Hello?" said Chuck in response to the pick-up. "Is this Patricia Hendrich?"

He hit the record button on the tape recorder, capturing the woman's voice.

"Yes, who's speaking?"

"Um, never mind who I am. If you want a name, how about this one... Basil Hendrich. Huh? Ring any bells?"

The woman sounded irritated. "Is this the Maury Povich show again? Look, I told you people..."

Chuck hurried to correct her. "No, no! Christ, no. Nothing like that. I'm just calling to say we have your father."

There was a very long stretch of dead air with no response. I half expected her to hang up.

"Your father, Basil Hendich," Chuck added, hoping that might clarify things.

"My father is dead," said Patricia Hendrich across the long-distance connection.

"Yeah, I know. We've got him."

"What do you mean, you have him? He's dead and buried. I was at the funeral."

"I'm sure you were. But we dug him up and now he's ours."

"What load of crap is this?"

"No really, it's true."

After a moment of thought, Patricia Hendrich switched her tone from irritated to skeptical.

"Prove it."

"Prove it?" asked Chuck, caught off guard. "What am I going to do, put him on the phone?"

"Why would anyone want to dig up my father?"

A fair question with an unfair answer.

"For ransom," Chuck told her.

"You're trying to ransom off a dead body?"

"Sure, why not?"

"What kind of idiot are you? No one pays ransoms for dead bodies."

"Sure they do," Chuck assured her. "Sometimes. To keep them from being—I don't know—desecrated or something."

"Look, assuming this bullshit is for real, I'd need some kind of proof before I'd even consider coughing up a single dime for what's probably a prank call."

Chuck can think on his feet, I'll give him that much.

"Um, proof. Okay. Well, sure. Do you have an address, like a post-office box or something we could use?"

> **Day of the Jekyll** (1979) 101min. U.K. Director: Ronald Furst, Cast: Basil Hendrich, Alice Kent, Peter Zane, Fiona O'Neil, Tom Jennick. Basil Hendrich takes his turn as the doctor with a potion-drinking problem. His make-up as the horrible Hyde leaves much to be desired, but his performance hits a high-water mark for scenery chewing. O'Neil is lovely, if short-lived, as the showgirl who draws unwanted attention from Jekyll's bad side. ***

Chuck set down a heavy toolbox and opened it to search through the hammers and nails and screwdrivers for something that would get the job done. At last he selected a pair of cutting pliers and walked to the couch where Basil sat. He selected one of his fingers—his right index—and grabbed hold of it with the pliers.

"Don't worry, Basil," he told the corpse, "you won't feel a thing."

Chuck squeezed the pliers hard, trying to separate the first joint of the finger from the rest of the hand. It was harder work than I would have guessed.

"So how is this not desecrating a corpse?" I had to ask.

Chuck strained to complete his task, squeezing the grips of the pliers with both hands.

"It's one finger, okay?" he said in his defence. "It's not even a whole finger, just a tip. Enough to get a decent print off of."

"Cut it at the joint," Steve suggested as he watched Chuck struggle. "Less bone to go through."

Chuck took Steve's suggestion and altered his angle of attack. Moments later there was a sickening crunching noise. I tracked the severed digit with the camera as it fell and rolled across the floor. Steve retrieved it from under the couch.

"Even if we courier it, that's still a whole day," I pointed out. "We can't leave a dead body sitting on your couch forever."

"He's embalmed," shrugged Steve.

"So what?" I said. "That doesn't do shit. He'll still rot. He'll just look prettier while he's doing it."

"No, Vince is right," Chuck said to Steve. "For once. We have to put him on ice."

It took us half an hour to chip all the frozen dinners out of the chest freezer that filled much of the laundry room not already occupied by the washer, dryer and water heater. We dumped all the packages, along with a stack of steaks and one large turkey, onto the floor to thaw and spoil.

"Think that's enough room now?" asked Steve.

There was still a fair amount of accumulated ice and frost taking up space inside, but with some bending and stuffing, we managed to squeeze Basil's body into cold storage. Chuck confirmed Basil's head was low enough to allow the lid to close.

"That's got it," said Chuck. "An inch or two of headspace to spare."

"What do we do with all this stuff?" I asked of the pile of frozen food.

"Toss it," said Chuck. "The TV dinners all taste like cardboard anyway."

"And the bird?" Steve asked, picking up the frosty turkey like a malformed bowling ball.

"My mom buys one every year thinking she'll cook it for Thanksgiving," said Chuck. "As if."

Steve dropped the turkey into the garbage bag Chuck held open for him. It took three more to wrap up all the abandoned meals without overloading the bags to the point of tearing.

> **Cannibal Cataclysm** (1978) 100min. Italy/ U.S.A. Director: Pasquale Marro, Cast: Edoardo Vicari, Claudia Bellizzi, Serena Ditta, Aurora Tosto, Basil Hendrich, June Colver. Despicable euro-exploitation trash sees young dubbed exchange students running afoul of a tribe of lost cannibals in the jungles of Brazil. American horror veterans Hendrich and Colver appear in obvious inserts as concerned parents trying to buy their daughter's freedom in talking-head scenes that literally phone it in. Shorter versions excise all the (real) cruelty-to-animals footage. BOMB.

Steve and I stood outside the storefront of a courier company, shooting Chuck through the windows as he hunched over the counter to fill out a shipping slip for a small package. He finished his transaction, paying in cash, and joined us outside.

"You made up a fake return address and phone number, right?" I asked, eager to confirm Chuck was playing things smart.

"Nah, I gave 'em a real one."

"Chuck..." I cautioned him, not in the mood to be kidded.

"Do I look stupid? I gave them the number and address of a pizza joint I don't even go to."

"Would you like Italian sausage or human finger on that?" quipped Steve, but nobody laughed.

"It should be there bright and early," said Chuck.

We drove around town the next day, looking for a different pay phone, just to be safe. There was one sitting on a street corner on a block with more boarded up shops than open ones. Chuck planted his microphone on the receiver again and recorded the conversation when Patricia Hendrich answered.

"Well it's definitely real," she concluded after they got the opening unpleasantries out of the way. "But how am I supposed to know it's my father's."

"Check the fingerprint," said Chuck.

"Right," she said, not masking her contempt. "Because I keep a handy-dandy crime lab in my pantry."

"Look," Chuck instructed her, "just dip it in ink, press it down on a piece of paper, and compare."

"Compare it to what?"

"Whatever's on file. Take it to the cops."

"Didn't you tell me 'no cops'?" Patricia asked, referring to the final note of her last conversation with Chuck.

"Don't tell them what it's for."

"My father's never been arrested," said Patricia. "Even if the police gave people off the street access to their files, they're not going to have his fingerprints floating around on some database."

Chuck lowered the phone from his ear, threw his head back, and sighed. He banged his skull on the booth glass for good measure. Composing himself, he returned to the negotiations.

"Well, what the hell else do you want as proof?"

> **Chop Till You Drop** (1977) 91min. U.S.A. Director: Morris Lutz, Cast: Gerry Barragan, Deloris Aikins, Basil Hendrich, Bernice Koepp, Rosanna Buckle, Dick Buscher. Gruesome horror "comedy" features plenty of gore effects and not a dash of wit to go with them. Poor excuse for gallows humour involves the boss of a meat-packing plant who decides unionizing employees would be better off as prime rib. Gore hounds will appreciate the work of F/X artist, Bud Schiller, which is the only thing to recommend this rubbish. Also known as "Give 'em the Axe!" and "Vile Cutlets." *

Back home, the tool box came out again. This time it was a hack saw that was pressed into service.

"Oh no," I told Chuck when I saw his next instrument of bodily destruction. "No, no, no."

"What difference does it make?" he asked in all sincerity. "We already chopped off a finger."

"*We* didn't chop off anything," Steve corrected him. "That was all you."

"And I'll do this one myself too," Chuck assured him, sounding a tad superior, I thought. "It's just a slightly bigger piece. What's the big deal?"

"You don't see a problem with this?" I asked him.

"It's a solution *to* a problem," he stated. "Look, your moral objection has been duly noted, okay? But once we deliver the body, all the various bits and pieces will be reunited, and everybody's happy."

Chuck marched into the laundry room with the saw. I didn't follow. This was an escalation I didn't care to capture on camera. But the microphone picked up the sound of it just fine. It was the sound of sawing—metal teeth grinding their way through ice and flesh frozen solid. And the sound went on and on and on until it became unbearable.

"How's it going in there?" Steve had to ask at last.

I got up to take a peek through the open door with the camera and got a shot of Chuck straddling the freezer, hunched over the frosted interior, working the saw hard on one limb he'd pried away from the rest of the body.

"He's frozen right through and it's not making it any easier, that's for damn sure," he told us.

I backed away to give Chuck and Basil their privacy. Less than a minute later, the sawing stopped at last, punctuated by what sounded like a brick landing on the tile floor.

"You got it ready?" called Chuck from the laundry room.

"Yeah, ready," Steve confirmed.

Steve held a large bubble envelope open for Chuck as he emerged from the laundry room, dangling the disembodied right hand of Basil Hendrich by the middle finger. Steve extended the yawning receptacle at arm's length so Chuck could drop the frozen block of flesh inside. I thought he looked a touch squeamish as he pulled the plastic strip away from the lip of the envelope and sealed it.

"I hope this does the trick," said Chuck. "All this dismemberment is costing me a fortune in courier fees."

> **Frankenstein in the Flesh** (1976) 96min. U.S.A. Director: Brad Winnock, Cast: Stephen Hardick, Beatrice Colm, Genevieve Rousseau, Basil Hendrich, Grant Moore, Isabella Frume. A retelling of the age-old tale for the sexual politics of the '70s. In this one, the "monster" isn't a misshapen horror, but a buff and handsome hunk, stitched together from the choice bits of virile young men. Apparently designed to make up for the mad doctor's inadequacies, things get out of control when his creation runs amuck, seducing every woman in sight. Or are they the ones seducing the innocent man-child? Hendrich makes up for missed opportunities of the past, finally getting to play Dr. Frankenstein to the hilt. He doesn't seem aware of the sexually explicit nature of the scenes he's not in. **

"Well it's definitely a real hand," Patricia Hendrich conceded. "And the finger fits."

We had found one more public pay phone to cram into and record our latest exchange with the target of our extortion plot.

"So are you satisfied?" Chuck asked her.

"I don't know," she said, sounding like she was still debating our legitimacy as grave-robbing blackmailers. "There aren't really any distinguishing marks."

Chuck sounded incensed. "Who else's hand could that be? Look at those bony fingers! He strangled six victims in *Motives of a Killer* with that hand. Hell, it was the lead monster in *The Crawling Fear* once it got cut off in the sawmill accident and developed a mind of its own."

"I haven't seen any of those stupid movies," said Patricia.

"You haven't?" asked Chuck, alarmed by the idea that Basil's own flesh and blood might not be as intimately familiar with the great man's career as he was. "Why not?"

"I really don't care to," she simply said.

"Well that's not my problem. Rent a DVD and see for yourself."

"Maybe if you sent his other hand," Patricia began to suggest.

"No!" Chuck was adamant. "No more body parts! We keep that shit up, you'll have the rest of him by next week."

"All right, fine," Patricia sighed. "I believe you have his body. The cemetery left a message on my machine yesterday. I haven't spoken to them yet, but I can guess what it was about. What do you want?"

"That's more like it," said Chuck.

Finally he was getting somewhere. But now that he was there, he wasn't sure what to do next. After a brief pause, Chuck put his hand over the mouthpiece of the phone and consulted with us outside the booth.

"What do we want?" he asked us.

When Steve and I both hesitated to answer, Chuck made a snap decision and returned to the conversation with his own figure.

"We want a million dollars. Cash."

The gales of laughter coming over the phone line were so loud, it was like Patricia Hendrich was standing in the booth with us.

"Is there a problem?" Chuck asked, once the commotion died down enough for him to get a word in.

"I figured you must be an idiot to have come up with this scheme, but now I know you're dreaming in Technicolor. A million dollars? Who do you think you dug up? Howard Hughes?"

"There must have been an inheritance," Chuck speculated.

"Oh sure," she said. "He left me his cat. You want it? You can pay the vet bills, be my guest."

"Well, I suppose we can listen to any counter offers you might have."

> **Reno Runs Red** (1973) 112min. U.S.A. Director: Samuel Yellen, Cast: Jarvis Derrick, Heddy Grammar, Drew Filstrum, Basil Hendrich, Jack Laxer, Penny Dupris. Yet another entry in the post-Godfather glut of gangster movies. The boys with bent noses crack out the tommy guns to resolve disputes about money, territory and women. Bloody, violent, but diverting. Just don't get too attached to any of the characters. Despite the catchy title, most of the action takes place in Las Vegas. **1/2

"Ten grand?" asked Steve in disbelief.

"Yeah," Chuck confirmed.

We were walking down the street, leaving the booth far behind. Steve had been turning the figure over in his head since Chuck first announced it after he got off the phone. Any way he totalled it, the math didn't add up to much.

"That's it? Ten grand?"

Even dead, Basil Hendrich should have been worth more to someone. Anyone. Especially his surviving family.

"It's ten grand more than you've got," Chuck reminded him.

"Split three ways," I was compelled to point out.

"It's not getting split any which way," insisted Chuck.

"Hey, we're a part of this too," said Steve.

"Yeah, you are," agreed Chuck. "We're all co-producers on this project. And as producers, it's our job to come up with the cash to pay for it."

"Are you kidding? This is the cheapest-ass movie anyone's ever made. Even the big star is working for free."

"There's still going to be post-production. Film transfers cost money. Burning DVDs costs money. Web hosting costs money."

"This is extortion, you know," I said, reminding Chuck that his entire financial structure was based in illegality. The kind that could send us all to jail.

"Patricia Hendrich isn't the victim of an extortion plot," Chuck said. "She's an investor in a feature-film production."

"Try telling *her* that," I said. Steve and I may have been willing to get wrapped up in Chuck's fantastical view of what we were doing, but I doubted anyone else would see it his way. Patricia least of all.

"Maybe I will when I see her," said Chuck.

"What do you mean, 'see her'?" asked Steve.

"We have to deliver the body in person."

This was news to us.

"We do?" said Steve.

"Why?" I asked.

"Because this film doesn't have a big enough budget to afford overnighting the star in a giant bubble envelope!"

"Okay, take it easy," said Steve. "When are we doing this?"

"Now," Chuck announced. "Let's chip Basil out, stuff him in the car, and hit the road. If we leave right away, we can beat rush hour and be there in a couple of hours."

Colonel Piggyback (1971) 88min. U.S.A. Director: Skip Whistle, Cast: Jenny Cambridge, Wes Killam, James Freznick, Basil Hendrich, Coleen Usher, Tutu the Wonder Dog. Hippie-dippy sex-n-satire artifact purports to mix politics, social commentary and sexual liberation into a cohesive whole, but nothing sticks. Members of the Hollywood old-school show up to play the disapproving authoritarian kill-joys. Muddled, confused and trippy, I'm sure it's fantastic after a hit of acid. Anybody sober should stay away unless you're required to sit through it for a social-studies class. *

"Clear!" I called out after using the camera to survey the street and the zoom lens to inspect possible trouble spots. Aside from a single backyard dog pacing behind a slatted fence, there was no movement. Nobody to witness us moving a body from one crime scene to the next.

At my signal, Chuck and Steve burst through the screen door of the house, one on either side of a frozen-stiff Basil Hendrich, fixed in his freezer-friendly sitting position. They rushed him down the steps to Chuck's waiting car. The doors were already open and they were able to quickly and efficiently stuff Basil into the back seat and tuck him in.

"Shotgun!" Steve called, trying to claim the front passenger seat.

Chuck immediately shut him down.

"Camera gets shotgun. You're in back."

"You sit next to him," Steve complained. "He's fucking freezing."

Chuck was already behind the wheel and I had joined him in the front. With no other options, Steve reluctantly claimed his chilly seat next to our celebrity star.

"I'd let Basil drive before I trusted you behind the wheel of my car," said Chuck. "Dead men earn no demerits."

"How many are you up to now?" I asked Steve, who had clocked almost as many demerits as miles since he first started driving.

"Thirty-seven," he said without having to add them up in his head. "They haven't taken away my licence or anything."

"I'm sure that's a bureaucratic oversight that will soon be corrected," said Chuck as he began to back us out of the driveway.

I noticed a thin layer of steam rising off of Basil's frozen body as the top layer of frost melted. Steve hugged himself against the cold and looked miserable.

"I'll leave the sun roof open," said Chuck magnanimously. "He'll thaw soon enough once we're on the road."

"Hopefully not too soon," I cautioned. "The meat has to stay fresh for delivery."

Chuck wound his way through the suburban maze of streets until he found the nearest boulevard. The open road lay ahead.

> **Go Fish** (1969) 126min. Canada. Director: Angus McCree, Cast: Colin Mercier, Jayne Woodrick, Guy Laroche, Audrey Burns, Basil Hendrich, Travis Meadows, Brent Underwood. Earnest low-budget drama about Newfoundland cod fishermen and the unforgiving sea is the cure for insomnia but serves as a worthy example of regional filmmaking. At least the scenery is compelling. Ill-advised cast awkwardly mixes amateur locals and seasoned pros and answers the question: how many ex-pat Canadians can be airdropped from Hollywood and still have the movie qualify for a tax credit? **

"You got a problem?" Chuck asked me suddenly.

We hadn't been on the highway more than five minutes when he posed the pointed question. I noticed his eyes had been on me more than the road, and apparently he didn't care for the expression he found on my face.

"I just don't like having him around," I said.

Inanimate object though he may have been, I felt Basil's presence was throwing off the usual group dynamic of our trio. That plus, of course, he was dead and had become the focus of a criminal conspiracy.

"What's not to like? How often do you get to chill with a celebrity?

"Yeah, but he smells," I replied, hoping to draw attention away from my deeper misgivings and towards a certain off tinge that hung in the atmosphere of the car.

"He does not smell," Chuck insisted. "He's embalmed."

"And frozen," Steve was quick to remind me.

"He's still going ripe," I said.

Perhaps what I thought I could smell was only the anticipation of decomposition, or merely freezer burn, but the usual smells of Chuck's car—junk food, oil leaks, and a heater that stank of scorched plastic—were lost under a more oppressive scent I could taste in my mouth and feel on my skin.

"He was in the ground for a day," Chuck said. "Tops. He's got a ways to go before he starts to stink."

We drove for a few more moments in silence. I cracked the window on my side, but the air that slipped in only succeeded in stirring the odour, not venting it.

"There!" I practically shouted when I saw Chuck react. "Smell that?"

"That's not him."

"That's definitely him!"

"Bullshit. Steve, smell him."

Steve balked at the order. He was already closer than he cared to be.

"The fuck I will."

"That's not rotting-corpse smell," Chuck maintained. "That's your own B.O."

"Stop the car," I demanded.

"No way," was Chuck's answer.

"Stop the car, I'm not going another mile in this stink."

Steve leaned forward and stuck his head into the middle of our argument.

"Chuck, pull over here," he said.

"I'm not letting him out," said Chuck, referring to me, not our dead hostage. "You said it—we're in this together."

Steve pointed out a convenience-store gas-pump combo off the parallel service road.

"Service station," he explained. "Just for a minute. We'll get some gas and some potato chips for the road and we'll work out a compromise."

> **Hysteria** (1968) 95min. U.K. Director: Rudolph Guiller, Cast: Basil Hendrich, Michael Orlando, Catherine Dobbs, Petunia Carlson, Jim Cole. Solid psychological thriller with no budget but plenty of atmosphere. Londoners are being driven mad by something lurking in the fog. Could it be devils, poison gas, or mass delusion? Intrepid police inspector, Hendrich, is on the case. Intelligent writing and credible performances make up for other shortcomings. ***

Ten minutes later, we were back on the road, taking an exit south. A pine-scented air freshener was now dangling from the rear-view mirror.

"Happy?" Chuck asked, not sounding like he cared in the least.

"Over-fucking-joyed," I told him.

In truth, the bag of potato chips did more to mask the corpse stink in the car than the air freshener did.

"So where's the drop point?" Steve wanted to know, crunching his way through another handful of salt-and-vinegar flavoured grease.

Chuck was hesitant to answer.

"I've been meaning to talk to you about that," he said at last.

"What's the deal?" I asked, not bothering to mask my dread.

"Basil's daughter runs a shop in a little town in Upper New York State."

"Whoa, wait a minute!" exclaimed Steve. "New York? We're crossing the border with a corpse?"

The state of New York was very close, but we were still in Quebec. It wasn't just another state or province, it was a whole other country.

"I'm not crazy about the idea either," said Chuck, "but it has to be done."

"Can't she meet us halfway?" I asked.

"Oh, sure," said Chuck with disdain. "Like how she met us halfway on the ransom. We're lucky she didn't ask us to bring him around to her house and stuff him in the mailbox."

"Don't you think it's going to look a little suspicious?" Steve asked. "Customs agents are all super paranoid as it is."

"Maybe we can hide him in the trunk," I speculated aloud.

"We can't put him in the trunk," said Chuck. "They always check people's trunks at the border because they think you're trying to smuggle in Mexicans."

"Mexicans?" asked Steve, unconvinced. "From Canada?" "They're very sneaky, those Mexicans."

> **Across the Rio Grande** (1968) 119min. U.S.A. Director: Dwight Clemens, Cast: Buck Wilkins, Basil Hendrich, Jamie Hernandez, Marie Yokum, Chad Devries. A trio of Texas Rangers keeps the peace around their backwoods town. Mostly by shooting Indians and Mexicans alike with impunity. I guess they're supposed to be the good guys. Who knows anymore? Okay western that was already past its prime the day it was released. **½

We were parked on the shoulder, half a mile up the road from a busy highway border crossing. Dozens of cars were lined up at each of the gates, waiting their turn to be questioned by customs agents before being let through. This was in less draconian times, just a few short years ago, when you could still drive across without much hassle. Now you practically need your birth certificate, a recent blood test, and cavity search. Not that I'll ever know. I expect I'm blacklisted from cross-border travel forever in the aftermath of my last visit to the States. I can only hope our escapade wasn't one of the things that got the border tightened, and turned crossing it into the miserable experience it is now. If it was, count that as another thing I'm deeply sorry for.

Chuck stood on the hood of his car and observed the scene. Even in those kinder, gentler days, he didn't like our chances of smuggling a corpse across in plain view.

He hopped down and announced, "Yeah, it's a no-go. Too busy."

"Busy is good," Steve suggested. "Busy is perfect. They'll probably just give us a pass."

"Unless we get pulled aside for a random check," I said. "Then we're fucked."

Three young guys in a car, even with an elderly chaperone, were likely to have some dope on board somewhere. We were low-hanging fruit waiting to be picked by an agent looking to up his quota of drug busts. They wouldn't find any pot stashed in the glove compartment or taped inside the wheel well. It's what else they wouldn't find that would make it a quality collar for them—a pulse coming from the fourth occupant in the car.

I didn't have to say anything else. Chuck was already on the same page.

"There won't be anything random about it. Three twenty-something guys in a shit car? We might as well be doing lines off the dashboard and handing out pro medical-marijuana fliers."

"You got a plan?" asked Steve. "I'd love to hear it."

"Everybody knows if you want to sneak some contraband across the border, you don't go through one of the big highway checkpoints. You look for some little backwater border-town crossing."

Chuck went around to the passenger window and reached into the glove compartment for the map.

"All those guys do all day is wave folks through from one end of town to the other. A monkey could do that job, and that's just about what they hire to do it."

Chuck flicked his wrists and let the map unfurl in the slight breeze like a table cloth. He spread it over the roof of the car and began to hunt through the endless criss-crossing blue veins that ran, unnamed, through the vast white expanses of cartography, away from the clearly marked and numbered arteries.

"Just look for the smallest dot you can find on the 49th."

My Name Is Bomb, Jamie Bomb (1967) 93min. Italy. Director: Fernando Rio, Cast: Niccolo Ajello, Angela Viscusi, Mauri Pacella, Basil Hendrich, Douglas Raffelton, Susan Thatch. Quickie Italian comedy/spy-thriller meant to cash in on the Bond mania of the '60s. Bad dubbing can't save bad acting in an international-intrigue plot that doesn't even try to make sense. Keep an eye out for a handful of Hollywood players slumming for quick cash and (presumably) a free vacation in Italy. The title says it all: BOMB

"Yeah, this'll do nicely," said Chuck.

We'd been discreetly observing a much smaller border crossing for the last ten minutes. In all that time, not a single vehicle had passed through. It stood on the outskirts of a tiny town we couldn't even find a sign to give a name to and was little more than a glorified toll booth. There was an American customs agent to handle traffic heading south on one side of the road, and a Canadian agent on the other side doing the same for northbound vehicles.

"What if they ask to see I.D.?" I asked.

"That's okay," said Steve. "We've got our Medicare cards."

"We don't need a passport. Yet," Chuck added.

"I'm not worried about us. I was thinking about him," I said, reminding them of our cargo.

"Basil doesn't need I.D." Steve smiled. "He's famous."

"Yeah," I agreed, "which makes it worse if he's recognized. All we need is Basil getting spotted by someone who watches enough Access Hollywood to have heard he's dead."

"That's not Basil Hendrich, okay?" said Chuck. "That's my granddad. We're taking him to see his sister in Vermont and the old guy's dozed off. And yeah, people tell him he looks like Basil Hendrich all the time. He finds it very flattering and I'll be sure to tell him you thought so too when he wakes up from his nap."

"That's our cover?" I asked, unconvinced.

"It's simple," said Chuck, starting the car. "Simple is good. Simple works."

The time for discussion was over. We were already pulling up to the gate for the American crossing. Chuck rolled down his window and greeted the uniformed agent.

"Hi there!" he said pleasantly.

The agent was already typing Chuck's licence plate, viewable in his booth through angled mirrors, into his computer terminal. He was all business, by-the-book, and didn't acknowledge Chuck's greeting.

"How long will you be visiting the United States of America?"

"It's just a day trip," said Chuck. "We should be coming back sometime tomorrow."

The customs agent's eyes shifted constantly from our faces in the car to whatever data was appearing on his computer screen.

"Is the purpose of your visit business or pleasure?" he asked.

"We're seeing family," lied Chuck. "Not much pleasure in that."

Chuck tried to laugh at his own joke, but the agent was too much of a hard-ass to respond.

"Are you carrying any firearms, tobacco, prescription drugs?"

"No, nothing," said Chuck, who decided it was best to keep the jokes in check.

"What's with the camera, son?" asked the agent.

I was caught off-guard by the question directed at me. I'd been shooting the transaction the whole time, largely unconscious of doing so. Having dutifully documented each stage of our escalating crime, each new law we had broken, it had become second nature to capture everything.

"Just shooting some home movies, sir," I answered, as politely as I could. I hoped my simple explanation would satisfy him. It didn't.

After a lengthy period of him typing on his keyboard for no discernable reason, the agent finally told us, "Step out of the vehicle, please."

Chuck looked at us like a condemned man and then opened his door to get out of the car.

"And the others," added the agent.

We all got out and stood next to the car. Only Basil didn't move. Obviously. The agent dipped his head down so he could look at Basil in the back seat and address him directly.

"You too, sir."

That was all it took to make Steve panic.

"Okay, we're lying!" he confessed on the spot.

Chuck spared Steve a poisonous look, but he already had the customs agent's undivided attention.

"We're not visiting family," Steve told him. "We're a television news crew."

I picked up Steve's lie where he left off.

"Yeah," I agreed. "We're doing a report on border security for the CBC. That's what the camera is really for."

"You know," Steve prompted the agent, "hidden-camera report? Only, it's not really hidden."

"Hidden in plain view," I said. "It was our director's idea. He thinks he's clever."

Chuck shifted his venom-dipped gaze to me, but said nothing as the agent took a moment to chew on this new story. We all waited to see if he would swallow.

"See bee see?" he said at last.

The fact that he didn't fully understand what we were telling him seemed to help make our bullshit sound authentic.

"Yeah," Chuck said. "Nobody in Canada really watches it either."

Now that we had the customs agent on the line with a whole new lie, Chuck ran with it.

"Anyway, we've done reports in the past about how security has been tightened, post nine-eleven. You know, the usual song and dance. But this time we're looking to profile the brave men and women on the front lines who protect us all from..."

Chuck struggled to think who we needed to be protected from. Steve and I tried to help him out.

"Migrant workers," I suggested.

"Cross-border shoppers," said Steve.

Chuck had a sudden epiphany.

"Oh, and, you know, terrorists. Guys like that."

The border agent only stared back blankly, so Chuck took that as an invitation to continue.

"Would you be able to take some time off for a sit-down interview?"

"You want to interview me?" said the agent, who sounded skeptical at best.

"Yes," confirmed Chuck.

"For television?" asked the agent, unconvinced.

"Absolutely."

"On the see bee see?" said the agent, who not only sounded unconvinced, but also unimpressed.

"You got it!" enthused Chuck.

The silence was thick in the air as the agent tried to digest this giant dose of manure. At long last, his reply came.

"How's my hair?"

"Perfection," Chuck told him.

"I'll have to call someone to get this okayed," he said. "You stay put."

The customs agent stepped back into his booth and picked up a land line that directly connected him to some higher authority.

"That's CBC," Chuck called after him. "Let me know if you need a spell check on that."

While the customs agent was distracted on the phone, Chuck began to inch back to the car.

"We should go," he said.

"What about the guy on our side?" asked Steve. "He's watching us."

I turned the camera for a shot and a look. The Canadian customs agent was eyeing us suspiciously from his booth across the road.

"Fuck him," said Chuck. "Our guys don't even have guns."

Chuck hopped behind the wheel and we followed, piling in and shutting the doors as quickly as we could pull all our limbs inside. The engine roared to life and, with an abrupt jolt of acceleration, Chuck turned sharply and drove the driver-side wheels up on the curb so he could squeeze the car past the gate that was still down. It was a tight fit, even for a compact, and the tip of the gate's arm dragged itself along the right side of the body, scratching the hell out of the paint job as the car forced its way through.

A moment later we were clear and racing into rural New England. I pointed the camera at the passenger-side mirror, watching the border crossing diminish behind us. I could see the tiny figure of the customs agent running out of his booth to watch our car escape his sphere of influence.

"They arm the American agents though, right?" I asked, mostly as an afterthought.

"Well yeah," said Chuck. "Of course."

The customs agent struck a pose—legs spread, arms forward—and pointed something down the road at us. I could just make out the miniscule flash of light from the point where his hands were raised. A fraction of a second later I heard a loud crack and the side mirror I'd been looking into shattered and sent shards rattling against the passenger door of the car.

"Oh fuck!" was the best I could come up with in the moment following the impact of a bullet less than a foot away from my head.

I ducked down in my seat amidst the shouts of dismay and confusion from my companions and, for several long high-speed moments, shot nothing but shaky unusable footage of the vinyl upholstery until I had the sense to shut the camera off.

Bullets Are Cheap But the Ladies Cost Plenty (1966) 112min/83min. Italy. Director: Domenico Mitro, Cast: Elia Monetti, Gabriella Stabile, Thomas Cancilla, Cyril Depace, Basil Hendrich, Jeremy Benz. Spaghetti western/comedy blows its load in the genuinely thrilling opening sequence. After the titles, it's shooting blanks. Jokes and gunplay abound, but nothing hits the mark. Severely cut for American distribution, maybe the longer cut makes more sense. Also released as "Gun? What Gun?" and "Django Laughs and Loves." *½

By the time I deemed it worthwhile to turn the camera back on, we were driving down a densely wooded back road. It was paved, with two lanes, but well off the highway with no other traffic in sight.

"Is anyone following us?" Chuck asked for what must have been the tenth time.

"If there is, we probably lost them a few turns back," assured Steve, as he kept a vigilant watch out the back window.

Chuck had been taking every random turn offered to him since we blew through the border, until he was satisfied he had no idea where we were. I think the logic was that if he didn't know, nobody else would either. It didn't stop him from stealing paranoid glances over his shoulder every few seconds, despite the fact that Steve was already observing the road behind us, and he had a perfectly functional rear-view mirror in front of him.

"You sure?"

I pointed the camera at the miles of empty road behind us and zoomed in to the horizon, looking for any other cars or blinking lights.

"There's nothing back there," I confirmed.

Chuck was still half-turned in his seat when Steve, eyes forward, screamed in sudden terror.

"Chuck, watch it!"

Both of Chuck's feet were on the brake before he could even see what the road ahead held, but it was too late. A moment later, the camera was wrenched from my hand as we came to an abrupt, violent halt. There wasn't a crash so much as a tremendous curt bang. My head snapped forward, my arms and legs whipped in front of me like banners in a wind storm. I had a brief flash of cubes of shattered safety glass floating in the air in front of me, and then I lost consciousness.

> **Yargh!** (1965) 88min. U.S.A. Director: Ben Wishman, Cast: Rod Lerman, Gloria Schleicher, Zach Fitts, Basil Hendrich, Marlene Kenyon, Majorie Mann, Quintin Hoose. Rubber-suited monster terrorizes bikini-clad beachcombers in this drive-in fodder that's

every bit as terrible (and hilarious) as its title and concept would suggest. Cult favourite among bad movie aficionados, it's a must-see for them and a must-skip for anyone else with sense. BOMB

I wasn't out long. It was the force of the collision and my seatbelt pulling tight across my chest that had knocked all the air out of me. There was no head trauma I could detect, but my skull throbbed just the same. I could hear groans inside the car, only some of them my own. Steve was wheezing in the back, suspended by his own locked seatbelt. If it weren't for the ingrained habit of buckling up, even after running a border crossing and being fired upon, we'd both be dead. Chuck fared better, but he was dealing with a face full of airbag. In his minimal-option car, his was the only seat equipped with one, but now it had him pinned.

"Is everyone all right?" I asked.

"Think so," said Chuck into the airbag.

"Ow. Ow. Fuck. Yeah," answered Steve.

Either shock or instinct made me reach for the camera where it had landed on the floor. It was covered in broken glass, but it was all from the car, none from the camera itself. It appeared to be in good working order, but I couldn't say as much for myself. I opened the passenger door and tried to step out, but my feet wouldn't work and I tumbled onto the pavement amidst the wreckage strewn all over the road.

Chuck managed to unbuckle himself and get out from under the inflated bag that was taking up most of the wiggle room on the driver's side. He reached back and helped Steve find the button to release his own belt. It was only then that he noticed something was missing.

"Where's Basil?" asked Chuck.

We all looked around for the fourth occupant in the car, but he simply wasn't there. Steve was the first to spot him.

"Aw, shit!" he declared.

We followed his gaze, through the shattered windshield, far down the road that lay ahead of us. Basil was sprawled across the white line a good twenty yards away, having been launched out of his seat by the high-speed impact.

Chuck put his shoulder to his door a few times before it finally wrenched open and he came spilling out on his side. Steve scrambled after him. We all stood up on unsteady feet and surveyed the disaster. Only once my head stopped spinning and I was able to stabilize myself did I notice the copious amount of blood that was trickling out from under the front half of the car. The entire hood had been accordioned by whatever had stopped us cold.

"What the fuck is it?" I asked.

Chuck staggered to the front to assess the damage to his vehicle, which was, as far as I could judge, totalled. There was a huge pair of antlers poking above the exposed engine block at the point of contact.

"Moose," declared Chuck, observing the gigantic animal. "We hit a moose."

"Is it dead?"

Steve joined Chuck at the front of the car and called it.

"Yeah, it's pretty goddamn dead all right."

"Jesus," I said. "We killed a moose."

Chuck wasn't so moved by the demise of the magnificent woodland beast. He was far more traumatized by the state of his ride.

"Fuck the moose," he yelled, "he killed my car!"

"You said it was a piece of shit anyway," I reminded him.

"But it was *my* piece of shit!"

Steve paced back and forth by the side of the road, his eyes darting from the wrecked car, to the moose, to Basil, and back again. He looked like he was having an anxiety attack. It sounded like a good idea and I considered joining him.

"Aw, Dude!" cried Steve.

"I know," agreed Chuck.

"Dude!"

"I know."

"Seriously, Dude!"

"Shut up!" Chuck yelled at him. "I know, okay?"

"Are we sure we're all right here?" I interjected. "No head injuries?"

I was pretty sure I was okay, but I wasn't so certain about Steve. He made a concerted effort to calm himself down and felt around his scalp with his fingertips, searching for a concussion.

"I'm fine," he announced.

"No internal bleeding?"

Steve and Chuck both felt their sore ribs where their seatbelts had stopped them.

"No. I don't think so."

"How's Basil?" was my next question.

We all turned towards our fallen star. His limbs were twisted in freaky, unnatural ways that suggested multiple breaks and dislocations. Even from a distance we could see the expanding pool of liquid forming around him.

"Not so good," declared Chuck.

He and Steve started to march towards the body.

"What's that leaking out of him?" I called to them as they got closer.

"Embalming fluid, I guess," reported Chuck.

"Help me get him up," he told Steve.

Chuck flopped Basil over onto his back and took him by the arms. Steve bent down, grabbed the legs, and together they tried to lift him. Only a few inches off the ground, Basil's arms detached from his torso, sending Chuck falling back on his ass with both of them in hand.

"Oh, this is beautiful," said Chuck.

Steve stood up straight again, holding one of Basil's legs by the ankle. It, too, had pulled free and come spilling out of his pant leg. The stump trailed a thin stream of chemicals onto his shoes.

"Fucking beautiful," Chuck added.

Chuck tossed the pair of arms down in frustration and disgust and hid his face in his hands.

"I guess he should have buckled up," commented Steve.

"You think?"

"Oh God," I said, thinking I might be sick.

Unable to watch or shoot anymore, I turned and walked to the back of car, putting some more distance between myself and the dismemberment.

"Fuck! Would you stop moving him!" I heard Chuck bellow behind me and was compelled to turn back again. I regretted it immediately.

Chuck was holding Basil's severed head in his hand. He pointed it accusingly at Steve.

"Look at this! Look at this! What I am supposed to do with this?"

"Oh my God," I said again, this time knowing I would have to be sick.

I leaned against the back of the car with my head down, gasping for air, but nothing would come up. I was still waiting for the vomiting fit that refused to happen when Chuck appeared at my side and unlocked the trunk. He dug around in the mess inside and came up with a couple of large, empty sports-equipment bags. Bringing them back to the scattered bits and pieces of Basil Hendrich, he threw one to Steve.

"Start packing," he instructed.

> **Six Shooters Ride Again** (1964) 112min. U.S.A. Director: Sterling Taylor, Cast: John Johnston, Eddie Bishop, Andre Fesser, Basil Hendrich, Paul Russell, Patrick Highsmith, Janet Sommers. Third entry in the Six Shooters oeuvre marks the point where the series starts to outstay its welcome. Hendrich, Russell and Highsmith fill the ranks for the Shooters who were killed off in the previous film. Spoiler alert: none of them return for the next entry, "Six Shooters Ride South." Competent western dust-up, but tired. **½

The two bags sat in the road, zipped tight and stuffed full of Basil. Chuck was crouched behind the car and, with a final twist of a tool he'd also salvaged from the trunk, removed the licence plate.

"There," he announced, "Now it's just another abandoned car."

"The border guy entered your plate into the system," I reminded him. "They know we were the ones who ran the gate."

"You sure?"

"He wasn't sending joke emails to his border-patrol buddies."

"Good point," admitted Chuck. "I'll report the car stolen as soon as we get home. Three crazy kids with some old guy as the ring leader."

I shook my head with as much disbelief as I knew the authorities would.

"That won't work."

Steve was standing in a field a short distance from the road. He called to us.

"Guys?"

Chuck didn't listen to him any more than he did me.

"Sure it will," he insisted, with baseless optimism.

"Guys!" Steve shouted, demanding our attention.

We turned to look and saw that Steve had moved closer to the edge of the nearby woods. We followed his gaze up above the tree line and, far in the distance, saw a helicopter flying low, making a sweep over the forest. We could hear it as it drew nearer. It was hard to say how far off the speck in the sky was, but it was getting louder.

"You think they're looking for us?" said Chuck.

"Yeah, I think they're looking for us!" was Steve's assessment. "No shit they're looking for us! We're going to have a fuckload of border security up our asses in another five minutes!"

"Okay, everybody off the road," Chuck ordered.

I hopped the drainage ditch that ran next to the two lanes and ran through the grass towards the trees. Chuck grabbed one of the bags of Basil and was right behind me.

"Steve! Get the other one!" he barked.

Steve was reluctant to return to open ground but did as he was told. I was closer, but was already burdened by the all-important camera. Snatching the second bag, he threw it over his shoulder and made a break for the woods. The three of us crashed into the brush a moment later, forcing our way through brambles and branches that scratched at our faces and snagged our clothes. Once we were through to the older growth, the going was easier, but we had lost valuable time fighting our way into the timber. The helicopter was much louder now and getting close. They must have spotted the car and were coming in for a better look. The growth of trees was thick enough to offer us complete cover as we wove our way deeper, getting ourselves as far away from the scene of the accident as possible.

The noise of the churning helicopter blades grew unbearably loud. It must have been hovering right overhead. I looked up, but there was nothing to see but branches and leaves being blown about by the powerful downdraft of air. We ran, and kept running, until we could run no more.

The Wandering Eye (1963) 88min. U.K. Director: Terrence Gains, Cast: Basil Hendrich, Lucy Davies, Todd Murdoch, Sandra Leigh, Benjamin Toffler, Arnold Bolt. Hendrich hams it up as a disfigured ophthalmologist who goes mad after losing an eye in a grisly fishing accident. When bodies start piling up the question is posed: who is murdering the good doctor's patients, him or the headlining disembodied eye? Forgettable grindhouse fare, but a treat for bad-continuity fans who will notice the main character's eye patch switches eyes in several shots throughout the movie. **½

Things were much more quiet and peaceful in the middle of the woods—or what we assumed was the middle of the woods. We could only guess how deep we were. The only noises were bird calls and the steady crunch of dry leaves and twigs underfoot. Chuck and Steve lugged one bag each as I brought up the rear, documenting the hike that had already dragged on for more than an hour.

"If they catch us like this, they'll probably shoot us on sight," complained Steve. "They're gonna think we're a bunch of Al-Qaeda terrorists sneaking around looking for shit to blow up."

"Oh, come on!" said Chuck. "We're exactly what we look like."

"Graverobbers and extortionists?" I suggested.

"We're suburban white kids hauling our asses through the woods with sports-equipment bags. What they're going to think is that we're a bunch of Canuck dumbfucks who got lost on the way to a hockey game."

"Well it's a hell of a way to break into the film business, that's all I can say," groused Steve.

We walked in bitter silence for a few moments until I tried to lighten the mood.

"Hey guys."

Chuck and Steve stopped and turned. I lined up both their faces in a tight two-shot.

"Look, *Blair Witch*," I said, and jostled the camera up and down.

By the time I stopped, Chuck had an angry finger pointed in my lens.

"Knock that shit off!" he snapped. "It's bad enough this whole thing is hand-held, you don't have to shake the camera on purpose!"

"Okay okay," I muttered, deferring to the artistic vision of my director. "You don't have to be such a bitch."

I didn't want to say anything, none of us did, but the day was getting on and we didn't want to get stuck in the woods after dark. Not that I thought there was much in the way of ravenous wild animals to worry about this close to various towns and freeways, but we were already lost enough. After a night sleeping on the ground in pitch black, we'd probably head out the next day and end up walking in circles. I wasn't so sure we weren't already doing exactly that.

It was another ten minutes before we found the path: a muddy trail used by hikers in more seasonable weather. Even though the path was just as deserted as the rest of the woods, it had to have been travelled enough to stay clear, and popular enough to justify building the bridge. It was a simple structure of planks over concrete supports, but it forged a narrow river and kept the feet of local joggers and dog walkers dry. The bridge lay in the direction we guessed was south, so we took it, assuming the path on the other side led somewhere, anywhere better than where we currently found ourselves.

As we crossed, I hung back for a moment to observe the babbling water below. It was hardly a gushing torrent, but I got the idea that it might be sufficient to destroy evidence. I didn't hear Steve double back until he caught me dangling the video camera over the river by its strap. He snatched it from me before I could let go.

"What the hell are you doing?"

"Nothing," I claimed.

"You nearly dropped it, you bonehead."

"Yeah, like that would have been a tragedy."

"You were going to do it on purpose!" accused Steve, cradling the camera close to himself, like he was protecting an infant from the big bad world.

"It's evidence, you moron!" I hissed at him. "It's going to be Exhibit-A at our trial!"

"It's Basil's last movie!" Steve growled back at me. "Show some respect!"

"Respect?" I said incredulously. "We dug up his corpse! We've been dragging his dead ass around everywhere for days! Now we've taken him on holiday and we've reduced the man to..."

I tapered off, trying to vocalize precisely what we're reduced him to.

"...to luggage!" I concluded.

Steve looked down at the heavy bag in his other hand.

"Okay," he agreed, "it's all kinda gone to shit on us. But don't take it out on the film. It's all we've got out of this mess."

Steve must have seen enough shame in my eyes to trust me with the camera again. He handed it back and I accepted the responsibility once more.

"Besides," he added, "frankly, at this point, I think it can only help us. It's evidence we weren't trying to commit an even bigger crime."

Chuck, otherwise oblivious to our exchange, called at us from the other side of the river.

"Hey, come on! Quit jerking off, there's a road here!"

The Fantastic Professor Fitzwater (1962) 95min. U.K./U.S.A. Director: Albert Collett, Cast: Basil Hendrich, Richie Gust, Lyndon Nickles, Peggy St. Laurent, Lincoln Fischbach. Science-fiction fantasy for the kids (big and small) showcases the imaginative inventions of the wacky professor as he and his students are whisked away on a series of grand adventures to impossible worlds. Beloved in its day, modern kids will find the cheap sets and practical effects clunky. Still a nostalgic treat for their parents who probably grew up watching it over and over again on television.
***

The motel wasn't quite what I would have classified as civilization. It was a mile or two too far down the highway from the main drag to qualify, but with the sun setting it was a most welcome vision. I set about my assigned task of pounding on the ice-machine button repeatedly, trying to fill the supplied bucket. No matter how many times I pressed it, it refused to fill more than halfway. Feeling dry after our long hike, I sucked on a small chunk of ice while I waited. It was enough to see me through the next few minutes until I had access to a tap and a glass.

At last Chuck emerged from the front office carrying both bags of Basil in one hand each. A room key dangled from a plastic number tag clenched between his teeth.

He spat it into my ice bucket and announced, "Okay, I got us all a room."

"One room?" I asked.

"Yeah, why?"

Once we were outside Number Four, he dropped the bags, retrieved the key, and unlocked the door. There were only two single beds in the room.

"So which two of us get to cuddle up together?" was my next question.

"Hey, I paid for the room," said Chuck. "You and Steve can get cozy tonight."

"Ew," was my only response to that suggestion.

"You want your own bed, get your own room," said Chuck, dragging our luggage inside.

"Cheap bastard," I said under my breath.

His money, his rules. He'd been the only one with the foresight to bring a stash of U.S. cash with him when we hit the road. Of course, he was also the only one who knew we'd be crossing the border.

Chuck took the bucket from me and surveyed the meagre contents, disappointed.

"That it?" he asked.

"Ice machine crapped out," I explained.

Chuck unzipped one of the bags and dumped the frozen shards onto Basil's remains.

"Never mind. I sent Steve to the corner store for Freezie-Sips."

On cue, Steve passed by the open door and stepped inside when he saw it was us. He had an armful of plastic shopping bags, all of them stuffed with frosty junk food.

"We're good," he told us. "I cleaned out their entire stock."

Steve dumped his loot across one of the beds. Chuck stuffed the frozen packs into the second sports bag and topped off the first with the leftovers.

"They were all out of cherry," Steve apologized.

"He doesn't care what flavour they are!" said Chuck, zipping the bags closed again.

"So what's our next move?" I asked.

Berlin Must Fall! (1961) 157min. U.S.A./ U.K. Director: Greg Merle, Alston Figg, Cast: Dudley McCasky, Orval Bye, Vince Corning, Kendall Malley, Basil Hendrich, Edmund Cornforth, Stuart Ferry, Dion Mcquay. All-star, all-male cast exhaustively (and exhaustingly) retells the final days leading up to Germany's surrender at the end of WWII from both the Allied and Axis sides. A touch too self-important with about a dozen too many scenes of old men gravely looking at maps, but lively whenever it gets back to the battle lines. A veritable who's-who of its era, with far too many familiar faces to mention. Only a few of them get to really shine. ***

Chuck called for a taxi from the front desk and together we cabbed it into town. Typical of New England, the two lanes of highway passed right through the centre of town and functioned as the main street for the short distance it took to travel from one end to the other. Chuck had the driver let us out in the approximate middle and paid him while Steve and I looked around, soaking in quaint Americana.

The brief stretch of the main was where every shop and commercial business was located, mostly in picturesque repurposed buildings from early in the town's history. There were only a few examples of contemporary architecture, although I imagined there was more of a mix in the residential suburbia that stretched back from the highway up streets on either side.

"Hey, check it out," Steve said to me.

There was a repertory movie house across from us that must have dated back to the days of travelling vaudeville acts. The marquee outside listed the show times for a number of oldies.

Chuck finished his transaction and our cab pulled away. He looked up at the lettering on the lit sign and declared, "Well I'll be goddamned."

"What?" I asked, not seeing what they were seeing.

Chuck read one of the titles advertised on the marquee, "*The Poison Pen of Doctor Death* is playing at the rep."

"Um, okay?" was my clueless response.

"Come on!" Chuck prompted me. "Poison Pen? Doctor Death? Who have we been hanging out with?"

Chuck looked at Steve for support, but got little more than a blank stare.

"I haven't seen it either, actually."

Chuck looked disgusted with the both of us.

"1957, black and white. Basil plays a family doctor who gets called in to pronounce one of his patients dead. Only he figures out it was murder, and instead of reporting it, he uses the evidence to blackmail the killer. Things go badly after that. Very cool. Never seen it on the big screen, though."

Chuck stared longingly at the venerable cinema for too long, and Steve had to resort to physically dragging him away to our real destination.

"Hey," he protested, but submitted to putting business before pleasure.

We didn't have to walk far before we found the one and only local flower shop. We staked it out from a distance and could see a woman behind the counter serving a customer who was buying something pink and potted.

"That her?" I asked.

"Hard to tell from here," said Steve.

"Give me the camera," said Chuck.

Chuck took hold of the camera and used the zoom to get a telescopic view of the woman's face. As best as I could determine, she was pushing fifty and appeared to be trim and attractive, if a bit hard-looking.

"Yeah," decided Chuck. "She looks about the right age. Definite family resemblance."

"When are we meeting with her?" Steve asked.

"Right now," said Chuck, zooming the camera back out and returning it to me.

"What? Now?" I asked, suddenly unnerved by the promise of a confrontation that could get ugly.

"Tuck that thing under your arm," he instructed. "Don't make it obvious you're shooting."

With the angle now a little lower, I followed Chuck into the shop, openly carrying the camera but pretending I wasn't filming anything at the moment. The three of us sniffed around the inventory as casually as we could. There was a curtained partition in the back and I made a point of poking my nose and camera lens behind it to see what was there.

The tiny room was filled to overflowing with flowers and three enormous men who were busy creating aesthetically pleasing arrangements to suit specific occasions and orders. They looked more like body-builders than flower-arrangers. In a different context, I wouldn't have looked at any of them and thought "flowers." I might have guessed bouncers or linebackers. Flower-arranging always struck me as a tad effeminate, but maybe they were gay—body-conscious work-out fanatic gay men who could snap my scrawny spine over their knees without breaking a sweat.

One of them caught me watching their work and looked up. The look wasn't friendly, it was menacing.

"Oops," I said. "Pardon me."

Leaving them to it, I let the curtain fall back into place. I turned around in time to spot the store owner, who could only be Patricia Hendrich, approach Chuck.

"May I help you?" she asked him.

"Oh, yes ma'am," said Chuck in stride. "I'm interested in buying some flowers. For my girlfriend."

Steve chortled at the mention of Chuck's imaginary girlfriend. He'd had a very long dry spell on that front, but it was his cover story and he was sticking to it. He flashed Steve a harsh glance that told him to stifle it.

"Certainly, sir," said Patricia. "What sort of arrangement do you have in mind?"

"I'm not what you would call a connoisseur," said Chuck. "My thumb's just about any colour but green. I was hoping maybe you could recommend something nice."

"Women always appreciate roses."

"Roses are good," Chuck nodded. "I could go with roses."

Patricia led him to the tall climate-controlled display case that filled an entire wall. There was a selection to choose from inside.

"Of course, there are many varieties," she explained. "And you have to be careful what kind you choose and how many."

"Why's that?"

"Different colours and different amounts mean different things."

"Like a code?" Chuck suggested.

"There are certain traditions to be aware of. For example, you wouldn't want to give your girlfriend two dozen red roses. Not unless you had an engagement ring to go with them."

"A couple dozen roses and she's going to want a ring on top of that?" Chuck said. "Sounds like an expensive date."

"I'm just saying, if she knows what two dozen red roses are supposed to mean, she might be disappointed if you don't follow through."

"Well why don't we cut the number in half and change the colour?" suggested Chuck. "I don't want her getting any funny ideas."

He pointed out the white roses.

"How about these?"

"White roses are certainly classy," nodded Patricia.

"Classy is good."

"But dull," she added. "Too pure."

Chuck looked Patricia in the eyes and asked her, "What do you like?"

Patricia took one step over and revealed a variation on the white roses. The tips of the petals were degrees of red and pink.

"These are my favourite," she said. "They're called 'minuit.' The class of the white rose, with a hint of passion around the edges."

"Sounds perfect," agreed Chuck. "What do you think, guys?"

He only got a series of hums and non-committal noises from Steve and me. It summarized our disinterest nicely.

Chuck smiled at Patricia and told her, "Wrap 'em up."

> **The Devil's Dynasty** (1960) 101min. U.K./ U.S.A. Director: Anton Thakkar, Cast: Vince Kiesling, Basil Hendrich, Maxine Boyd, Evan Mundt, Jeanett Havel, Craig Vogl. Paganism and witchcraft abound in a tiny seaside village as Christian crusaders try to figure out who needs to be burnt at the stake. Budget horror outing offers a deeper morality tale beyond the cheap thrills, suggesting nobody is guilt-less in the conflict between ideologies. Point taken, but it also gives us nobody to root for. General audiences will find the film unsatisfy-ing. Known in North America as "The Devil's Daughter" and "Satan's Son." ***

"What was the point of that?" I asked, once we were out of the shop and walking away down the street. Chuck had his freshly purchased bouquet of roses in hand, professionally wrapped in decorative paper.

"I wanted to take a good look at her," he said. "You know, before she finds out who we are and gets all pissed off."

"So was she everything you expected Basil's daughter to be?" asked Steve.

"I wasn't expecting anything. But she seemed nice."

"I guess," I said. "In a sales-clerk move-the-merchandise kinda way."

"I'm the first to admit, Basil's a sort of creepy-looking guy," said Chuck. "And I love him for it. But his kid turned out pretty okay."

"Oh, Christ," declared Steve, rolling his eyes.

"What?"

"'What?'" Steve echoed back at Chuck. "Come on, man, you're thinking she's a MILF."

"Get the fuck out!" said Chuck. "You know how old she must be? Do the math. She's more of a GILF. And I wouldn't, thanks just the same. Don't be gross."

"Right," nodded Steve. "Because you've got that hot girl-friend to go home to with all the flowers. What's her name again? Della something? Del...lusion maybe? That it?"

Chuck and Steve got into a playful shoving match which was all fun and games until one of them got shoved into me and sent my camera coverage wildly astray.

Before we'd made it to the end of the strip, we came across what was probably the only pay phone in town. Chuck stopped to make a call. He was immediately thwarted.

"You got any American change?" he asked us. "This thing is laughing at my Canadian quarters."

Steve dug into his pockets and came up with a handful of coins he got back from his Freezie-Sip purchase. Chuck helped himself and dialled. The exchange was brief when the other end picked up.

"The package has arrived," he announced. "Where do you want to arrange delivery?"

There was a short response Chuck agreed to.

"Okay, one hour," he said, disconnecting and giving us a thumbs up.

> **Invaders from Venus** (1959) 89min. U.S.A. Director: Shawn Pearse, Cast: Deandra Whitmer, Camelia Dutton, Jeffrey Huckstep, Parker Steffenson, Basil Hendrich, Jenni Newman. Earth is under attack, but our stalwart defenders are all too willing to roll over and take it once they get a look at the extraterrestrial invasion force (specifically their voluptuous figures). Don't worry, our heroes get the upper hand once they introduce the technologically superior shock troops to hitherto alien concepts like love, sex, and fumbling 1950s seduction techniques. Title aside, the titular invaders are actually from some other random planet beyond our solar system, but let's not get hung up on technicalities. **

We arranged ourselves at a table for four in a typical homey small-town restaurant. It was still early in the dinner service and there weren't many other patrons present—mostly families with children who needed to be in bed early. We had our privacy for several tables in all directions.

We'd only been sitting long enough to be brought a basket of bread rolls when Patricia walked in. She stopped at the "Please wait to be seated" sign and scanned the restaurant. It only took her a few moments to spot what she was looking for. Her eyes narrowed and she strode over to us without hesitation. Chuck half-rose from his chair for the lady, trying to be gentlemanly.

"Hello, Ms. Hendrich," he said.

"Big surprise," was her cold response.

Her ire was palpable. She probably knew who her earlier customers were the moment we walked into the flower shop. Chuck sounded disappointed his surprise had fizzled just the same.

"You guessed it was us."

"Guys don't buy flowers for their girlfriends in groups. They sneak in alone because they don't want to look pussy-whipped in front of their buddies."

Patricia looked my way next. Not at me, but directly into the lens.

"What's with the camera?" she asked.

"We're documenting the transaction for our records," Chuck explained in his half-bullshit sort of way. "Pretend it's not even there."

Patricia didn't need any additional prompting to ignore Steve, myself, or the camera. We were already beneath her contempt. She took the one available seat at our table, fired up a cigarette, and got down to business with Chuck.

"Where is he?" was the first thing she wanted to know.

"He's close," Chuck told her vaguely. "Do you have the money?"

"That's close too," she countered.

"You didn't bring it?"

"Do I look like I want to get murdered?"

"We're not going to hurt you," Chuck tried to assure her.

"I'll make sure of that," she said, and blew smoke from her cigarette up at the ceiling vents.

Our waitress, seeing our table for four was now complete, came over.

"Oh, we've already ordered," Steve told her.

We were hungry and hadn't waited for Patricia to join us. Somehow we figured she might not want to share a meal with us anyway.

The waitress ignored Steve and asked Patricia, "Ma'am, can I get you anything?"

"Coffee," she said. "To go."

"I'm sorry," the waitress began, "but there's no smoking in..."

"Fuck off, okay Denise?" said Patricia impatiently.

She wasn't reading the name tag on the waitress's uniform. Formality fell away as the everybody-knows-everybody reality of small-town life revealed itself.

"Patricia, honey," said Denise, showing genuine concern, "you all right?"

"I'm fine," said Patricia, taking another drag and making no move to put out her cigarette. She made brief, reassuring eye contact with the waitress and that was enough. Denise took the hint and gave us some space, trying her luck at another table.

"You know each other?" Chuck asked when we were alone again.

"We're all neighbourly here," said Patricia, and explained no more.

It became clear Patricia wasn't going to offer any small talk whatsoever, so Chuck asked, "When do you want to do this?"

"I talked to my bank today. I can get the cash tomorrow over lunch. There's a service lane behind the row of stores. Meet me there after closing."

Patricia stubbed out her butt on the empty plate at her place setting and rose. Chuck interrupted her abrupt departure.

"You didn't send flowers," he said.

It stopped her.

"What?"

"To your father's funeral. I didn't see any flowers from you on the grave."

Patricia settled back into her seat.

"No," she confirmed. "I didn't send flowers."

"Seems odd what with you owning a flower shop."

"I took a day off work to drive up and make a personal appearance," she said. "Not every sentiment can be expressed with an arrangement and a card."

Chuck reached down under the table and came up with the bouquet of roses he'd just purchased.

"I got these for you," he told Patricia.

"How sweet," she replied icily.

Patricia took them in hand and, as a bus boy passed with his cart a moment later, placed them unopened on top of his stack of dirty dishes.

"Could you throw these away for me, thanks," she said to him.

The flowers were whisked away to the kitchen for disposal and Patricia returned her cold gaze to Chuck. She lit another cigarette, like she was settling in for a lengthy stay, but said nothing more. Chuck took her silence as a challenge and broke it first.

"Look," he said, "I don't want to start off on the wrong foot."

"You already have."

"Right. Of course," he said, reminded of the nature of this transaction. "Please, Patricia... Can I call you Patricia? Or Pat? Patty?"

"My father called me Pat."

"Well then, Pat..."

"Patricia," she stated, cutting him off. "I hated being called Pat. It sounds like something you do to a dog."

"I have to be honest, Patricia," Chuck told her. "We're really just winging this thing."

"I thought you were professionals."

"Really?"

"No."

Chuck tried not to look deflated and continued.

"We had no intention of taking it this far. And no disrespect was meant. In fact, I'm really quite a fan of your father's work."

Patricia took a puff and asked, pointedly, "Why?"

Chuck shrugged, like the answer should be obvious.

"He was one of the giants."

Patricia stared at Chuck for a long moment, assessing him.

"How old are you?" she asked.

"I'm...in my twenties," answered Chuck as specifically as he cared to.

"Don't kids your age like..." she considered the state of Hollywood for a moment. "I don't know. Vin Diesel or The Rock or guys like that?"

"Come on," said Chuck dismissively. "Those guys suck. Basil Hendrich was the real deal. You'd know that if you'd seen any of his movies."

"Chalk it up to my deprived childhood."

"I'm going to guess you two weren't close."

Patricia had heard enough and cut straight to the point.

"What do you want from me?"

"I want to take you to a movie," said Chuck.

And for the first time, Patricia Hendrich looked surprised by something he'd said.

> **Wet Asphalt** (1958) 103min. U.S.A. Director: Lorenzo Baucom, Cast: Nicky Mosely, Margaret Baily, Basil Hendrich, Peter Olive, Marcell Parmley. Ernesto Vogan. Late-entry noir covers all the bases and delivers one of the finest examples of the genre since its heyday a decade earlier. Retired police detective gets handed a wad of cash and a mess of troubles when he's convinced to take one final tour of the urban underbelly of Manhattan to find a missing socialite. He doesn't like what he finds, but audiences sure will. Classic. ****

Chuck came back from the box office with a couple of tickets for the evening's screening.

"You'll like it, I swear," promised Chuck. "It's a classic mystery thriller. Really well done. Nothing cheesy or campy or any of that shit. In a way, I think it's his finest performance."

"Everybody's a critic," said Patricia, sounding disinterested.

"Your father was a great man," Chuck told her earnestly.

"I'm glad somebody thinks so."

Patricia flicked her cigarette into the street and followed Chuck inside.

"You're buying me popcorn," she informed him.

"Of course," he agreed.

Steve was at the ticket booth buying us a couple of admissions with the cash left over from his frozen-snack run.

"I want popcorn too," he called after Chuck.

"Buy your own goddamn popcorn," Chuck told him before disappearing inside with Patricia.

Once Steve completed his purchase and we had our tickets, we tried to enter the lobby but were stopped by an usher.

"I'm sorry, sir," he told me, looking at the video camera in my hand. "I can't allow you into the theatre with any sort of recording device."

"Are you shitting me?" Steve said in my defence. "This isn't a sneak preview. It's a fifty-year-old flick that's been on video and commercial television since before we were even born."

The usher remained firm.

"The rules apply to all screenings at this theatre."

"Chuck! Wait up!" Steve yelled over the usher's shoulder. "This ass-hat thinks we're pirates for the Chinese black market!"

But Chuck and Patricia had already passed through the lobby and into the screening hall itself.

"Forget it," I said. "I'm really not in the mood to see a Basil Hendrich movie anyway. You?"

"I think I've seen enough of the guy these last few days," agreed Steve.

"Chuck!" I shouted through the barred door. "We'll meet you after the show!"

By then, he was out of sight and probably out of earshot.

"He doesn't hear me."

"Fuck him," said Steve. "Let's go pound down a pitcher."

The town had only one of everything, and that included a single bar. But being the lone local, the place was packed. Steve and I found a tiny table in the corner and ordered a pitcher of whatever they had on tap.

"Cheers!" toasted Steve, with his first mug of beer.

"Bottoms up!" I countered with my own.

"To absent friends," Steve added, and tossed back a big slug of his brew. I followed suit and we both made the same awful face as we swallowed distastefully.

"Gah!" critiqued Steve. "Fucking American beer!"

Bad beer and bad music managed to kill a couple of hours. We left the bar in time to catch the cinema crowd as it let out after the show. Chuck and Patricia were nowhere to be seen, and it wasn't like it had been a packed house. It was the last screening of the day so nobody stopped us when we stepped inside to search the theatre for them. All the lights were on, and the only person left was the usher, sweeping up abandoned popcorn bags and soda cups.

"Where the hell are they?" I asked Steve, but he had no more clue that I did.

"Hey! I told you no cameras in here!" the usher shouted at us from ten rows away.

I got a good shot of him anyway, as well as Steve's arm extending into the frame to flip him off.

"Smile!" Steve shouted back before we fled.

> **Atom Monster-X** (1955) 82min. U.S.A. Director: Will Kincer, Cast: Warner Whiteman, Basil Hendrich, Inger Sax, Stefanie Prevost, Rudolf Rountree, Mariko Corpuz. Take one garden-variety salamander, add radiation, and presto—giant monster attack! Again. Another atomic-age beastie goes stomping on an iconic American city (this time Chicago) for no particular reason other than that's what scripts of the day required everyone and everything that grew to enormous size to do. Various normal-sized humans try to put a stop to it with a mix of science and romance. Haphazard stop-motion animation only serves to remind audiences just how great King Kong was a whole generation earlier. **

Short on cash, we strolled back to the motel along the side of the highway. It was more walking our feet didn't need that day, but there wasn't enough traffic flying by on either side to make it particularly perilous.

Back in our room, I set the camera down on the nightstand to await Chuck's return and report. He wasn't in yet, so Steve and I stayed up late, lying side-by-side in our single bed, watching scrambled pay-per-view porn on TV. It was all a little too close, a little too cozy, but we were both too tired to care.

"Maybe she didn't like the movie and they ditched early," I speculated.

"I didn't think wild horses could pull Chuck out of a movie before it was finished, but there's always a first time," said Steve.

"They're probably working out the finer points of the deal."

We fell silent as the headache-inducing signal on the television tinted the room with a sickening flickering light. The picture was an insoluble puzzle of distorted, tangled limbs we could barely comprehend, but the unscrambled sound offered enough cues to follow the plot which seemed to consist solely of moans and groans of sexual delight.

"Those squiggly blue people sure do know how to get it on," I commented during the current grind.

The positions of the coupling were already improbable. With the image scrambled, they were intriguingly impossible.

"Blue chicks are hot," Steve decided. "I could so go for a blue chick."

The rhythmic groaning and grunting quickened pace and seemed to fill the room with surround sound.

"They're really good speakers for a crap TV," I had to admit.

"We should totally pay to have this unscrambled," said Steve.

"Motel pay-per-view costs a fortune."

"So what? Chuck's playing the shot."

Steve reached for the phone on the end table between the beds.

"I'm gonna call the desk."

"Hey wait," I said, stopping him before he could press any buttons. "Mute it for a second."

Steve set down the phone and grabbed the remote control instead. As soon as he muted the TV, some of the moaning stopped, but not all of it.

"That's not porno," said Steve, listening intently.

"Sounds like somebody's having a party."

The noise was coming from the room next door, from the wall behind our heads. It was a couple, going at it at the same frantic pace as the professionals on TV.

"Fuck it," said Steve, leaving the television sound off. "This is better than the movie."

We eavesdropped on the intimate moment happening on the other side of a very thin partition. The sex grew louder, the pace became quicker, and the headboard thumping got harder—hard enough to shake our room's generic decorative-landscape painting askew. Steve and I joined in, acting as the couple's private cheerleading squad.

"Go! Go! Go! Go!" we encouraged with each thrust.

The thumping and grunting climaxed and Steve and I performed a two-man wave. There was silence after that.

"Was it good for you?" I asked Steve.

"Fuck yeah," he sighed.

House of the Werewolf (1951) 100min. U.S.A. Director: Nathanial Lines, Cast: Errol Karney, Basil Hendrich, Lilli Barren, Heidi Klassen, Raleigh Cullens, Sherman Condict.

More like "Wherewolf?" There's probably a moon-fuelled monster loose on the premises. There's probably a stack of bodies hidden away somewhere. Who really knows? Watch all the way to the end and you still might not know. Famously, we never quite get a good look at the shapeshifter in question. Cast and crew long maintained this was to add mood and keep their ambitious thriller from sliding into horror schlock. But it was probably a bottom-line decision to slash the makeup budget. Either way, the end results are notably mysterious and/or confusing. ***

Steve and I slept head-to-toe that night to avoid any inadvertent and unsettling spooning incidents. It was hot and uncomfortable and neither of us got much rest. It didn't help being jolted awake by a second round of hard, desperate sex in the next room.

Groggily, I felt around the floor at the foot of the bed and found a shoe to throw at the wall.

"Give it a rest!" I yelled, and tried to will myself back to sleep.

The Disturbed Grave of Dracula (1949) 98min. U.S.A. Director: Ron Nardi, Cast: Basil Hendrich, Vida Criddle, Paul Fleener, Rina Truby, Galen Hobbs, Michael Luckey. You can't keep a good vampire down. Not when there's money to be made from relentless rehashes. Okay as far as Dracula movies not derived from the source material go, but the Count should have more to do than biting necks and giving the slip to would-be slayers as per usual. The quickie finale tacked on at the end all but admits there will be another sequel (or ten) forthcoming. Followed by "Dracula Prowls the Night." **

Steve and I were roused by the grey light of dawn through the blinds on the window. And more fucking. The couple in the next room were at it again.

"Can you believe this shit?" I asked Steve.

He sat up, looking like crap. I probably looked no better. What little sleep we'd managed had been miserable and fitful.

"What time is it?"

I checked my watch.

"Way too early to be fucking that hard."

"Next time can we ask for a room that's not right next to the honeymoon suite?"

I noticed Chuck's bed was still made up. He hadn't been back, hadn't slept in it at all, while Steve and I had been crammed together in a single all night long.

"Look at this!" I remarked. "Chuck didn't even crash here."

"I slept with your stinky feet in my face when there was a perfectly good vacant bed two feet away?"

Our neighbours hit their latest peak and fell silent again.

"Maybe they're finally dehydrated," I suggested hopefully.

The phone in our room rang and Steve answered it.

"Chuck!" he said, when he heard the voice on the other end. "Where the hell are you? Yeah? Okay then. Are we set?"

Steve held the phone away from his face long enough to tell me, "We're confirmed for tonight."

"Okay, see you soon," he told Chuck and hung up.

"So what did he..." I began, but stopped when I detected the distinct sound of another phone being hung up. It had come from behind the motel-room wall.

Steve and I looked at each other as we listened carefully to footsteps crossing the floor next door. I grabbed the camera and joined Steve at our window as he parted the blinds. The door of room five opened and shut and Patricia Hendrich, wearing the same outfit from the previous evening, walked to a car parked in the motel lot and drove away.

"No way," said Steve, once the car had vanished from sight down a bend in the highway.

We hurried out of our room and went one door down. Number Five was closed but unlocked, and opened when we tried it. The interior of the room was a mirror-image layout to our own, with the furniture arranged in the exact opposite configuration. The only significant difference was the double bed compared with our own twin singles. It was a dishevelled mess, but didn't look like it was the only surface in the room to have played host to the sexual acrobatics of last night.

Water was running in the bathroom. That door wasn't locked either, so Steve and I let ourselves in. The camera lens fogged with the billowing steam from a hot shower.

"You forget something, babe?" Chuck asked from behind the shower curtain when he heard us come in.

Steve threw the curtain aside sharply, exposing Chuck, and we both let out a scream to ratchet up the shock. Chuck screamed back, in surprise and terror, until he realized it was only us.

"Fuckers!" he declared, as we laughed at his response.

Chuck stepped out of the tub, grabbed a towel and shut off the water.

"What the hell is this?" Steve asked him.

Chuck thought carefully for a moment before answering.

"End-of-second-act complication?" he ventured.

"Chuck, this isn't a goddamn movie!" I told him.

"Says the man with the camera."

Steve was laughing again.

"How could you?"

"I don't know. We were just talking," said Chuck. "And then the movie started and we were still talking. And people were telling us to be quiet so we left to go talk somewhere else."

"We didn't hear much conversation going on last night," I informed him.

"By the time we got back here, we were done talking."

"It's cool," snickered Steve. "Older chicks are hot."

Chuck tied the first towel around his waist and grabbed a second to dry off with.

"Let me tell you," he said, "she's got issues."

"Older chicks with issues," Steve nodded knowingly. "Double hot."

"She didn't talk you down on the ransom, did she?" I asked. "You know, for services rendered."

"For services rendered she should be paying us double," Chuck countered. "We're still set for our ten Gs."

"Tonight's the night?" confirmed Steve.

"Absolutely."

"How do we kill time till then?" I asked.

"Well," said Chuck, "I still haven't seen *The Poison Pen of Doctor Death* on the big screen."

Act Three

THE REPERTORY THEATRE reran its triple-feature schedule as a matinee. It was a handy way for a trio of sightseers in a town with no sights to see to kill an afternoon. There was hardly anyone else in the cinema, so we had our choice of seats. I documented part of the screening from the row in front of Chuck and Steve, shooting them munching popcorn and watching their screen idol in his prime—their screen idol who was now lying dismembered in twin hockey bags back at a dive motel up the road.

Steve reached over to help himself to more of Chuck's popcorn and had his hand slapped away for his efforts. I ducked down in my seat and hid the camera when I caught a glimpse of the authoritarian usher stepping inside to patrol the aisles.

The sun was going down by the time we emerged from six hours of screenings. Chuck had the cab that took us to our motel wait for a few minutes while we collected our luggage and checked out. With Basil loaded in the back, we had it take us back to town and let us off half a block up one of the side streets.

What traffic noise there was on main street faded away as we walked down the service alley behind the row of stores that included Patricia's flower shop. The sun was gone by then and the area was poorly lit after regular business hours. The restaurant and bar were both on the other side of the main drag. Everything on our end was closed for the night.

"Where is she?" Steve asked Chuck.

"She'll be here."

They both set their bags of Basil down on the pavement.

"Unzip them," Chuck instructed. "Let Basil air out a bit."

Steve opened the bags and withdrew quickly. Even before I could smell it myself, the look on his face told me Basil was beginning to spoil.

"Phew," said Steve, fanning the air in front of his face. "I think someone needs to get him back in the ground ASAP."

"We'll be done here soon," Chuck said.

"Heads up," I told them.

I'd already had the camera running, ready to capture the entire transaction. At the first sign of movement down the opposite end of the lane, I pulled focus, trying to do a competent job as our project's sole cameraman and cinematographer.

A lone figure approached us and we composed ourselves for the lady's arrival. Chuck greeted Patricia with a familiar smile when she stopped several paces in front of us.

"Hello, Patricia."

Patricia's response was abrupt and businesslike.

"Let's just get this done, please."

"How are you?" asked Chuck, trying to stay pleasant, cordial.

"Impatient."

Whatever had passed between them was indeed in the past. Chuck tried not to look hurt.

"Okay, then," was all he said.

"Where is he?"

Chuck motioned at the two bags that lay at our feet. If she hadn't noticed them yet, she must have been standing upwind.

Patricia looked momentarily confused, then crouched down and pulled aside the flap of one of the bags to have a look inside. She did the same for the second and stared up at us.

"What the hell did you sickos do to him?"

"He was like that when we found him," Steve exclaimed nervously. It was an obvious, lame falsehood, and it wouldn't wash.

"There was an accident," Chuck explained more truthfully. "I'm sorry."

Patricia continued to look in the second bag, calmly taking inventory, confirming the merchandise we were delivering.

"Looks like he's all here," she said.

"Well then, if you'd..." Chuck began. Patricia cut him off.

"Give me a minute," she said, her eyes fixed on the contents of the bag. "Let me have a look at the son of a bitch. I haven't laid eyes on him in at least ten years."

Patricia seemed focused on one particular item in the bag. I assumed it was Basil's head as opposed to, say, a melted Freezie-Sip pack. I might have leaned in for a better shot, but I wanted to give her her privacy.

"Didn't you see him at the funeral?" Chuck asked.

"It was closed-coffin."

"That's too bad. The embalmers did a beautiful job."

"Very lifelike," I agreed.

"Until we fucked it all up," added Steve.

There was a long silence that dragged on during this tear-less reunion. Nobody wanted to be the first to interrupt such a personal moment, but business was business.

"Satisfied?" Chuck asked at last.

Patricia stood up straight again.

"Not just yet," she said. "Boys."

I thought at first she must be referring to us, but a moment later the three burly flower-arrangers stepped out of the shadows from behind a row of dumpsters. They had been there the whole time, waiting, watching, listening. At Patricia's signal they made their presence known.

"So, about the money..." said Steve, even as he knew there would be no money forthcoming.

Chuck saw what was coming next. He didn't even try to resist when the first of Patricia Hendrich's thugs doubled him over with a punch to the gut. Steve tried to back away, but the second man floored him instantly with a shot to the head. I watched this happen through the lens of the camera. It made me feel distant from what was happening to my friends. It comforted me with the notion that the same fate wasn't in store for me, even as I turned and saw the third goon fill the frame. An instant later, I felt the first impact and the camera went flying. I saw it spin through the air and land on some trash behind a fruit and vegetable store. Juice and pulp-stained cardboard boxes broke its fall and saved our documentary from destruction.

I kept my eyes fixed on the camera, the red recording light shining in the dark, and the lens indifferently observing the brutal beat-down as the three of us got our shit kicked in by one flower-arranger each. We didn't try to fight back.

There was no point in pissing them off any further with token resistance. We just instinctively curled up into fetal positions as we were punched, pummeled and punted without mercy.

At Patricia's silent signal, the beatings stopped as abruptly as they had begun. The muscle men stepped back, leaving us all lying prone and in agony, groaning and cradling our bruised bodies as best we could.

Patricia stooped down to root through one of the bags.

"Ah, here it is," she announced, producing Basil's left hand.

"We could have avoided this entire transaction if only you'd sent me the other hand," she said to us. We were in no condition to respond.

There was a pinky ring on the last finger, quite small, quite modest. It was a simple piece of jewelry, easy to miss. And miss it we had. Patricia pulled it off and dropped the hand back in the bag.

She stood over Chuck and held the ring up where he could see it, assuming he was still capable of focusing on anything at all.

"Recognize this?" asked Patricia. She didn't wait for a reply. "The seal from *The Marquis Diabolique*. 1965. Dad's favourite role. It's the only thing worth a damn he didn't pawn off over the years. And did he will it to his only child? No, he wanted to be buried with it."

Patricia studied the ring under what little light there was, contemplating her inheritance.

"They say to be a truly great actor, you need to be ruthlessly selfish," she continued. "You're right, you know. He *was* great."

Chuck mustered the strength to speak, sputtering a few words between gasps for air.

"I thought...you said..."

Patricia answered before he could finish calling her on her lie.

"Of course I've seen all his movies," she said. "He was my father."

She carefully tucked the ring into the inside breast pocket on her jacket.

"Some movie fanatic will pay a fortune for this," she said.

She gave one of the bags a dismissive tap with the toe of her shoe.

"This rest of this shit is yours. Enjoy."

And with that, Patricia Hendrich turned and marched away, back down the alley. Her goon squad lingered long enough to make sure none of us were getting up again anytime soon, then followed her out.

We laid there on the pavement, not speaking, struggling to keep conscious despite our bodies' compelling arguments to give up and pass out. We listened to the departing footsteps until there was nothing to hear any more but the distant drone of the occasional car passing through town.

It took a long time before any of us could say anything intelligible. Chuck was the first to be able to form a complete sentence.

"I can't believe I didn't recognize the ring," he said.

> **Hitler's Spymaster** (1943) 97min. U.S.A. Director: Bertram Charters, Cast: Leland Hively, Josephine Fairbairn, Basil Hendrich, Haywood Gaskin, Gertrude Kitchell. Wartime

propaganda thriller takes on those dastardly Nazis who are out to steal the plans for America's super-secret Weapon Omega. The anti-fascist message is earnest enough, but Der Fuehrer's thugs come across as too cartoonish to be a serious threat to anyone. Badly dated now, and badly dated even back then once newsreel footage of the atrocities in Europe started trickling back from overseas.
**

We were in the woods again. Lost again.

Bruised and bloody, but nothing broken, we'd dragged our sorry asses out of town and managed to hitch a ride with a sympathetic truck driver who saw our swollen faces, black eyes and cut lips and bought our story that we'd been carjacked by bikers who had, for reasons obscure to everybody, suddenly decided to upgrade from two wheels to four by force. He'd let us off at a highway exit a few miles short of the border, and I'm sure he was glad to be rid of us. He was too polite to say anything, but our luggage stank. With the delivery of the body a no-go, we'd decided to bring Basil with us. It just seemed impolite to abandon him in some back alley.

We'd left the road as soon as the truck was out of sight, carrying the leaky bags into the woods, crossing country in hopes of finding a way back across the border far from the prying eyes of the authorities. Several hours in, we'd hardly said a single word to each other. It hurt to talk and we weren't exactly in a chatty mood anyway.

It was Steve who was first to break the silence, with a statement we were all thinking and somebody had to vocalize.

"I hope one of us knows where we are."

Chuck knew, or claimed to know. He at least knew what he was aiming for.

"Indian reserve. It's the best place to cross. No border cops."

"You sure about that?" I asked, not even certain which reserve Chuck was trying to navigate us through.

"Yeah," he said. "Reserves have their own police force."

Steve stopped walking and raised his hands.

"I noticed that," said Steve.

Chuck and I also stopped as soon as we saw what Steve saw. There was a uniformed cop standing in our path, pointing a rifle at us from a range that couldn't miss. A short distance behind him, parked on a dirt road, was a four-wheel-drive Range Rover, clearly marked as an official vehicle of the Mohawk Nation.

"You boys are a ways off from the nature trail," the rez-cop commented.

"Just tell us we're back home in Canada, please," said Chuck, too exhausted to come up with new lies.

"You're standing in one of the First Nations of aboriginal peoples," he announced, then added less formally, "Which is technically in Canada, yeah."

We all breathed a sigh of relief. But the rez-cop wasn't in the mood to welcome us home with open arms. He knew we were up to something—something no good. He kept his rifle trained on us.

"Drop the bags," he ordered.

Chuck and Steve did as they were told and tossed the bags to the ground with a heavy thud.

"You muling some drugs there, kid?"

"Does formaldehyde count?" replied Steve.

"What is it? Pot? Meth?"

The rez-cop stepped forward and leaned in. Keeping the rifle on us with one hand, he yanked the zipper down with the other and pulled one flap aside so he could see in. His reaction was instant, leaping back with both hands on his rifle again. He pointed the muzzle at each of us in turn, trying to decide who was biggest threat, which one of us might rush him and need to get shot first.

"Good Christ!" he exclaimed. "What are you? A gang of axe murderers?"

"Whoa, take it easy there, Navajo Joe," Steve said, keeping his hands in clear sight and trying his very best to look harmless.

"They're props!" Chuck yelled, trying to defuse the situation. "For a film."

Chuck pointed at the camera in my hand to back up his new inspired untruth.

"You're shooting a movie?" the rez-cop asked us. He looked skeptical, but a lot less likely to open fire.

"Low budget horror," Chuck said, flirting with the truth but still keeping it at arm's length. "It's all latex and stage blood. See?"

Chuck dabbed his finger to his swollen split lip and came up with some fresh blood. He held out his hand for the rez-cop to see. The constable slowly lowered his rifle, pointing it safely at the ground, and stepped up to have a second look in the bag.

"You're right," he concluded. "That does look pretty fake."

We three all exchanged a silent look, trying not to show any surprise that we were actually selling this story.

"So it's cool?" Chuck asked when it seemed we might get away without getting shot, without even getting arrested.

"You need a permit to shoot in these woods," the rez-cop informed us.

"How much does a permit cost?" asked Steve.

"How much do you have?" was the total we were given.

We exchanged another silent look. And then we all reached for our wallets.

> **Buzz Wingers** (1941) 106min. U.S.A. Director: Elroy Sprankle, Cast: Frankie Gilden, Ned Foxwell, Basil Hendrich, Brant Mooring, Lizabeth Branning. A feature-length re-edit from the Buzz Wingers serial that ran as weekly chapters the previous year. Entire subplots (also known as the slow bits) have been edited out in favour of more action and cliffhangers. Young daring bush pilots take crazy chances flying mail and other essentials to distant mining towns in the north and cross paths with a greedy land baron looking to stake everybody else's claim. Dumb fun whether in the air or on the ground, it only ever slows down for the token romance and a song or two. **½

It wasn't just Chuck footing the bill this time. The rez-cop had been perfectly happy to accept whatever Canadian cash Steve and I had on us. First-Nation reserve or not, it was Canada, and the currency was good. Good enough to buy us out of the current jam, at least.

As the rez-cop climbed back in his Range Rover with every penny to our name, Chuck asked him as pleasantly as he could, "Hey, can you give us a lift to the nearest bus depot?"

The rez-cop ignored him and pulled away down the dirt road, leaving us to suck on his dust trail.

"Thank you!" Chuck called after the departing vehicle, still staying pleasant. The cop may have just given us a shake-down, but he was the one with the gun. Best to keep the transaction civil. Bitterness was for later.

"What are we supposed to buy a bus ticket with anyway?" asked Steve.

"I still have my student Mastercard," Chuck said.

We stood on the dirt road for a while, looking up one end and down the other. There were no obvious landmarks to guide us or suggest a direction other than the phone lines that ran along poles set into the ground at even intervals.

"Which way to civilization?" I asked, once I was sure I had no idea.

"Left I think," said Chuck.

"My gut is telling me left, too," agreed Steve.

"Yeah. You should always go with your gut."

We stood there thinking about it for a few more seconds and then, without another word on the matter, all turned right and started walking.

Lost in Lebanon (1939) 75min. U.S.A. Director: Homer Hullinger, Cast: Joey Crayton, Max Friddle, Chelsea Hurley, Sarah Bargas, Van Rodman, Rene Pinkerton, Basil Hendrich, Hugo Roberie. Yet another entry in the "Lost in" series of musical comedies starring

Crayton and Friddle. This one ostensibly sees
the duo turned around and wandering
through exotic Lebanon (though it's obvious
they never leave the comfort of the back lot
except through the miracle of stock footage
and rear projection). Brimming with one-liners,
song-and-dance numbers, and contract players
in blackface. Amusing enough for its brief running time, but it was obvious they were out of
places to send the boys. Followed by "Lost in
Kashmir" and the mercifully final effort,
"Lost in Java." **

The brakes of the bus hissed loudly as it stopped at its station
to pick us up.

It had taken nearly three more hours of walking to get to
a town big enough to have a designated stop for a coach line
that would take us all the way back to the city. Chuck had put
three tickets on his card, making sure to remind us what we
owed him.

Once we were on board and on the road again with
wheels under us, it was amazing how short a time it took to
get back. The skyline was in sight not half-an-hour down the
road, and another half-hour after that saw us crossing the
bridge that took us home.

We waited on the platform of the city depot as a baggage
handler unloaded the luggage compartment from the belly of
the bus. No sooner did he open the hatch than he recoiled
from it, cupping a hand over his nose.

"Oh my God!" I heard him say under his breath.

Our fellow passengers gave the compartment a wide
berth as the handler dipped in to pull the first bag out. The

driver, seeing the reaction from the people he'd just delivered, came over to investigate.

"What's that stink?" he wanted to know. There'd been no such smell in the actual cabin of the bus.

"You hit a skunk or something?" the handler asked him with a hint of accusation in his voice.

Their discussion about what the source could possibly be continued as he threw bags onto the platform, one after the other. We quietly retrieved our two pieces and walked away, checking over our shoulders to make sure no one had tracked the smell to our luggage.

> **The Racketeers** (1937) 121min. U.S.A. Director: Myron Stanbrook, Cast: Alan Scher, Leona Weist, Cary Hankins, Susan Range, Les Dotson, Nanette Wilbert, Ray Stade, Basil Hendrich. Black market buyers and sellers are alternately pitied and condemned in this tear-jerker based on a magazine-article indictment of wartime wheeling and dealing on the civilian front. Lauded in its day, it did nothing to stem this sort of behaviour during the next conflict that would get rolling only a couple of years later. Basil Hendrich earns his first screen credit as a chatty gutter snipe who'll get you whatever you want, but never what you need. Little seen now, but worth keeping an eye out for on late-night cable and at the bottom of bargain bins. ***

"Look, it's on eBay already," said Steve.

He was sitting at Chuck's computer desk. Searching the web for any mention of our ordeal was the first thing he wanted to do, but there was nothing about a border breach or a car accident. Checking the online marketplace for signs of Basil's pinky ring had been an afterthought, but it was the only thing that got a hit.

We were all filthy from the trip. Cleaning our various wounds had been a higher priority for Chuck and me, but at the mention of the ring, Chuck emerged from the bathroom and looked at the digital photo of the prop jewelry that accompanied the sale. The provenance of the ring was summarized in the description that also gave all the pertinent details about the film it appeared in and its significance to the plot. There had already been interest, and the price was going up by leaps and bounds. Basil's death was still fresh enough in film-fan minds for collectors, casual or serious, to still be on the hunt.

"What's it going for?" Chuck asked.

"You're not thinking of making a bid, are you?"

"I might be," said Chuck sheepishly. "Maybe."

"You're a fucking idiot," I told Chuck with as much unblinking honesty as I could muster. He didn't try to disagree.

"Mmm," he conceded. "But I'm a fucking idiot who hasn't maxed out his credit card just yet."

Chuck's mom called from downstairs.

"Charles?" she bellowed in the sweet way mothers of adult children still call their name.

"Yeah, Ma?"

"Something smells!"

"It's the garbage, Ma! I threw out a bunch of TV dinners!"

"Well take it out, it's pick-up day!" she commanded, ending the hollering exchange.

The Yellow Press (1934) 78min. U.S.A. Director: Fred Vallens, Cast: Wendell Killam, Troy McTavish, Janine Munroe, Oliver Garner, Evelyn Unger. Fast-talking tale of journalists trying to out-scoop each other doesn't seem to know if it wants to be a screwball comedy or a hard-hitting drama. It swings back and forth with varying degrees of success, but at least it keeps moving. Look quick for a very young Basil Hendrich in his first feature-film appearance as a paperboy. **½

Chuck, Steve and I sat out on the front lawn of Chuck's house on a trio of collapsible deck chairs. We all wore sunglasses to protect our blackened eyes from the setting sun, and toasted our fallen comrade with swigs from bottles of beer as we watched our sad equivalent of a Viking funeral unfold before us.

The garbage truck approached, one address at a time, clearing the street of the week's trash that had been put out by neighbours for removal. We observed it like a spectator sport.

"I don't know what a test audience is going to make of this ending," I commented as I captured the last shot of the film.

I turned the camera to shoot the bags of waste sitting by the curb in front of us. Most were black plastic, filled with spoiled and expired food. The final two were polyester, stuffed with a very different type of spoilage.

"There are precedents for movies that end with the star getting crushed in the back of a garbage truck," Chuck commented sagely.

"James Woods in *Once Upon a Time in America*," suggested Steve.

"Mal Arnold in *Blood Feast*," noted Chuck.

"And Basil Hendrich in whatever the hell we're going to call this," I concluded.

"I've been thinking about titles," said Chuck. "I got one. It's perfect."

He didn't share it. I don't think he was ready to hear us shoot it down—ready for the compromise of collaboration.

"Well, I like it anyway," he added.

The garbage man working our side of the street saw us sitting there, tracking his every move as he threw the remains of Basil Hendrich into the back of the truck. He had to comment.

"What?" he asked us.

"You're doing a fine job," Chuck told him.

"Thanks, man," said Steve, raising his bottle of beer to him in salute.

The garbage man pulled the lever to trigger the scoop to come down and squash the latest load of trash. He hopped onto a stoop at the back of the truck and surfed it to the next door down, looking at us over his shoulder until he was clear of our unnerving presence.

"Goodbye, Basil," Chuck said softly and took a drink.

A few minutes later we were still watching the spot where the truck had rounded the corner and disappeared when a police car pulled up from the opposite direction. It wasn't a municipal cop car. This one was white with black and yellow highlights instead of the usual blue. There were two uniforms in the front and a couple of plain-clothes in the back. They all got out, but it was the plain-clothes who approached us. The uniforms hung back and remained watchful in case there was trouble. They conspicuously kept a hand on their guns.

"Charles Hardy?"

One of the detectives zeroed in on Chuck like he knew exactly who he was looking for and what he would look like when he got there.

We all glanced up from our deck chairs in response. None of us moved or said a word.

"I'm Detective McCullogh, RCMP," he announced and then introduced his colleague, "This is Detective Gagnon, Sûreté du Québec."

We didn't offer our own names. We'd already guessed they knew damn well who we all were.

"We'd like to have a word with you about an incident at the U.S./Canadian border two days ago," he continued.

"We were hanging out here all day," Chuck claimed.

"You drive a blue 1998 Honda Civic?" asked Gagnon.

"I did. It was stolen."

"Your car ran through border security," said McCullogh. "It's been impounded in Plattsburgh."

"You should look for those crooks there then," suggested Chuck. "Don't you think?"

"Suspects matching your description were also witnessed coming back through the Akwesasne reserve.

Steve failed to contain an incensed outburst.

"Son of a bitch! He took our bribe and then narced on us. Fucking Indian giver."

"Hey, that's racist," I was compelled to say.

"That's fuckin' accurate is what it is!"

McCullogh and Gagner kept things professional but firm.

"You're going to have to accompany us for questioning," McCullogh informed us. "All of you."

McCullogh took Chuck by the arm to make sure he rose to his feet without a struggle. He made no effort to resist. Steve and I followed his example.

"How deep a pile of shit are we in here?" Chuck asked, purely out of academic curiosity at this point.

McCullogh wasn't specific about the charges we faced, but in light of our cooperation he was candid.

"So far it's just provincial and federal. Plus the New York state police of course. But calls have been coming in from Homeland Security and the FBI."

"Oh yeah," he threw in an addendum, "And the U.S. Fish and Wildlife Service. Something about hunting moose out of season. Seems everybody wants a piece of you boys."

"Innocent till proven, right?" said Chuck.

"Sure," agreed McCullogh unconvincingly, turning Chuck around to put the cuffs on.

Chuck looked back at the arresting detective.

"You're a Mountie?" he asked.

"Yeah," confirmed McCollogh.

"Where's your hat?"

"We only wear those for picture postcards."

"We're making a picture right now," Chuck told him, and pointed his chin at me and the camera.

"You there," McCollogh ordered, "Shut that camera off."

I looked at Chuck for confirmation. He wasn't in charge here. Not anymore. But he was still my director.

"Uh, Chuck?" I asked, uncertain.

"Well?" asked Steve as Detective Gagnon was cuffing him, "What do you say Mr. DeMille? Did we get it?"

Chuck took a moment to reflect.

"Yeah," he said, "I think we might have enough material for a movie."

"Or a book," I suggested.

"Don't be stupid," said Chuck. "Nobody reads anymore."

A second provincial cop car pulled up, and another behind it. They were going to split us up, keep us from talking to each other, make sure we didn't get our story straight.

"I think it's in the can," were the last words Chuck said to me. "Cut it there. That's a wrap."

Filmography (No official release date or running time) Canada/U.S.A. Director: Charles Hardy, Cast: Charles Hardy, Steven Coolidge, Vincent Tremaine, Basil Hendrich, Patricia Hendrich. Only available to bootleggers and torrent-site pirates, this weird hodgepodge documentary appears to be evidence leaked from a sensational kidnapping and extortion trial from a few years back. You may remember the details. Legendary genre star Basil Hendrich (deceased) is dug up from his grave to "perform" in one last film. Rest assured, the irresponsible miscreants behind this plot are all doing time. If you're really interested, copies crop up for sale at horror conventions with differing amounts of footage. Hendrich's body was never recovered. Unrateable. It is what it is.

The End

Acknowledgements

The author wishes to thank Kathryn Presner, Ellie Presner, and Michael Brodie, for their eyes and assistance; David Lascelle and Mike Taylor for parking their asses on any number of couches and theatre seats right next to mine over the years; and the entire funeral procession of genre giants who are no longer with us, including such luminaries as:

Bela Lugosi (1882–1956)
Peter Lorre (1904–1964)
Basil Rathbone (1892–1967)
Boris Karloff (1887–1969)
Lon Chaney Jr. (1906–1973)
John Carradine (1906–1988)
Vincent Price (1911–1993)
Peter Cushing (1913–1994)
Donald Pleasence (1919–1995)
and Christopher Lee (1922–2015).

The world is, ironically, scarier without you.

About the Author

Shane Simmons is an award-winning screenwriter and graphic novelist whose work has appeared in international film festivals, museums and lectures about design and structure. His art has been discussed in multiple books and academic journals about sequential storytelling, and his short stories have been printed in critically praised anthologies of history, crime and horror. He lives in Montreal with his wife and too many cats.

Also by Shane Simmons

eBooks

Carrion Luggage
Choke the Chicken
The Red Baron: An Ace for the Ages

Graphic Novels

The Long and Unlearned Life of Roland Gethers
The Failed Promise of Bradley Gethers

Last Words

Small-press publishers rely on reviews from readers like you to help get the word out about their books. Whether it's a simple star rating or a written critique, every bit of feedback helps convince the impersonal computer algorithms of Amazon, and other literary outlets, that the book you just read has merit and deserves more exposure. Please support independent authors, editors and publishers by taking a few moments to share your thoughts and opinions with other potential readers who may be sitting on the fence about trying an intriguing novel or collection. Your suggestions or comments can make all the difference when it comes to helping them find a new writer they'll like, or matching a struggling author with the readership he or she deserves. Thank you.